Bizzybees:

A Science Fiction Novella and Two Short Stories

by

Harold Platte

hard sci-fi + philosophical sci-fi

*

a CatOnBall publication
First Edition ~ 2026

"Every civilization thinks it's asking the right question. Few notice they're answering one instead."

"We call it defense when we don't understand the invitation."

"If Bizzybees asks how we meet the unknown, the other two quietly demonstrate how badly we handle it."

"The shorter pieces are less stories and more controlled experiments—each one proving that misunderstanding scales faster than intelligence."

A signal appears. A world disappears. Something is watching Earth. When an unknown phenomenon erases a distant celestial body, governments scramble to respond. Weapons are deployed. Scientists are assembled. Panic spreads quietly behind classified doors.

Dr. Aram Namur sees something others don't. The Anomaly isn't attacking. It's waiting.

As humanity prepares for confrontation, Namur risks everything to prove a radical idea: First contact may already be happening—and we are completely misreading it.

But when the first probe reaches the Anomaly, the truth may arrive too late to change course.

For readers of intelligent, idea-driven science fiction.

Includes two additional short stories.

Bizzybees: A Science Fiction Novella and Two Short Stories
Author: Harold Platte

Published in 2026 by 'CatOnBall'

ISBN-13: 978-81-972055-5-2
First Edition

Edited and Set by Ujjwal Dey
Cover Image and Cover Design by Ujjwal Dey

Published by 'CatOnBall', an imprint of OdeWord.com in Mumbai, India. Visit us at CatOnBall.com for details. Published through Amazon KDP & print-on-demand services. Refer barcode for details of nation of origin and nation of printing. Disputes are subject to Mumbai, India jurisdiction only.

a CatOnBall publication
Visit us at www.CatOnBall.com

Bizzybees:

A Science Fiction Novella and Two Short Stories

*

hard sci-fi + philosophical sci-fi

Official Review from FreedomFiction.com

A quietly powerful work of science fiction that favors intelligence over spectacle, Bizzybees explores first contact not as conflict, but as misunderstanding. The novella unfolds with calm precision, revealing how easily humanity mistakes reaction for comprehension. The two accompanying stories sharpen this theme, each presenting encounters where meaning is present—but recognition fails.

Thoughtful, unsettling, and elegantly restrained, this collection asks a rare question: what if the universe is not hostile, but simply far more sophisticated than we are?

Foreword

There is a persistent habit in human thinking: when faced with the unknown, we assume it is either a threat or a puzzle to be solved. We prepare to defend, to classify, to respond. Rarely do we consider the possibility that the unknown may already be engaged with us—that it may be observing, waiting, or even communicating in ways we have not yet learned to recognize.

The works collected in this volume emerge from that tension.

At their surface, these stories belong comfortably within science fiction. They concern distant objects, improbable events, and systems that exceed present understanding. Yet beneath their speculative frames lies a more immediate inquiry: not what exists beyond us, but how we perceive what does.

The central novella, *Bizzybees,* unfolds as an encounter that humanity interprets through its most familiar instincts—reaction, defense, analysis. But the deeper movement of the narrative is not outward into space; it is inward, into the structure of human reasoning itself. What does it mean to interpret a signal? At what point does observation become assumption? And how often does action precede understanding?

The two accompanying stories extend this inquiry in quieter, more concentrated forms. They strip away scale and spectacle to examine something more precise: the conditions under which meaning is formed—and misformed. Each presents a situation in which intelligence is present, yet recognition fails. Not because information is absent, but because interpretation is constrained.

This is not merely a philosophical concern. It reflects a scientific reality. In every field—from biology to astronomy to information theory—we encounter systems that do not behave according to our expectations. Evolution produces outcomes without intention. Signals travel without guaranteeing reception. Complex systems respond in ways that cannot be predicted from their parts alone.

Human civilization, for all its sophistication, is no exception. It is itself a system—reactive, adaptive, often brilliant, and occasionally blind.

What these stories suggest is not that humanity lacks intelligence, but that intelligence alone is insufficient. To understand something fundamentally different from ourselves requires more than knowledge. It requires restraint, patience, and the ability to question the frameworks through which we interpret the world.

The future implied by these narratives is not defined by technological advancement alone. It is defined by a shift in posture—from reaction to reconsideration, from assertion to affiliation. Whether such a shift is possible remains an open question.

For now, these stories offer a simpler invitation.

To observe more carefully.

To conclude more slowly.

And to consider, if only briefly, that what appears incomprehensible may not be beyond understanding—only beyond our current habits of thought.

~ Ujjwal Dey
Editor, CatOnBall.com and FreedomFiction.com

*

Bizzybees

A Novella

#

Parallax sank Dr. Namur's stomach when the train on the opposite track began to pull away. Motion expected but not felt made him separate, briefly, from his stomach, though they rejoined after just a moment apart. *Enough,* he thought. The meeting at Brookhaven with the Department of Defense people had left him unsettled enough for the day.

Rows of white boats, lazing in the windless Potomac afternoon, began to move in the deeper distance when his train began, at last, to roll forwards. It had been his first time in Washington D.C. Few STEM degrees outside of the military had much occasion to visit in those final days of the era.

He had longed since the moment he left for the golden warmth of Richmond's soggy summers, where fuzzy sunlight wafted through wet well-pollenated air. Where Virginia trilled an echo of birds and insects, bloomed at all scales from lichens to soaring longleaf pines, spawned black beetles and fast fat-bellied spiders from the wet soil like condensation from thick grass, where Virginia had so much life and death and blooms and rotting, D.C. was one giant thing. D.C. was one organism. People like proteins, built buildings and dug subways, moving inwards during the day and outwards at night, the city respiring and consuming, sleeping but alive at night like the heart races in a nightmare, devouring sustenance from its suburbs and directing the flow of the world as a honeybee orders a thousand separate enzymes into a warm hexagon. D.C. carved itself a burrow and rested there, feeding, shitting, pulling in new branches from time to time, going out to kill its rivals or eat something's children.

What Dr. Namur learned at Brookhaven that week had just about stopped D.C.'s heart.

The adrenaline of individuals became the adrenaline of civilization as the discovery of what they simply called the Anomaly was transmitted through the social neuron channels from observatory, to observatory, to observatory, to military, to the appropriate decisionmakers, back to the military, and back to the observatories.

Neurons charge and release voltage potentials. This causes everything that happens to everything that knows it is alive. The observatories released their voltage potentials by transmitting the discovery of the Anomaly deeper into the amygdala of civilization, which charged and released its own voltage potentials in return, creating a loop that formed a thought-action. Civilization saw, processed, and reacted to the Anomaly, and by studying it, began to commit it to civilization's memory.

Dr. Namur was one person. He was one part of one neuron embedded within the Brookhaven cortex, an anterior processing gland of the midbrain of civilization. Doctor Namur's long academic career in the life sciences had accidentally made him the perfect interface between the processing-parts of the brain of civilization and the reacting-parts. The reacting-parts were already spinning up an uncoordinated, un-considered response: a reflex, absent all processor inputs, to redirect asteroid-deflectors laden with fusion bombs towards the Anomaly. From the perspective of the reacting-parts of civilization, there was simply no reason not to. The probes would take weeks to reach the Anomaly even at maximum acceleration, leaving plenty of time for processor-consideration, and when it comes to fusion bombs, it is always preferable to have them and not need them than to need them and not have them.

Namur's briefing materials horrified him. The convulsion of adrenaline throughout the brain of civilization caused by these reports was mirrored, in intensity if not in speed, by the adrenaline surge Namur himself experienced upon reading them.

The Anomaly devoured 385571 Otrera early in the morning, D.C. time, on the tenth day of summer. This was noticed almost as soon as the bright flash of light reached the Earth, seen first by automation tools and then promptly confirmed by human observers.

A leading trojan, 385571 Otrera orbited the Sun at the L4 Sun-Neptune Lagrange. Without a dedicated satellite or probe tasked to this relatively obscure Neptune trojan, no close-up video existed of the event itself, though the tiny pinprick of light that actually arrived at the Earth could be magnified and enhanced from the passive scans of surface observatories.

Further processing revealed that 385571 Otrera had not exploded. It had been replaced by the ring of light that came to be known as the Anomaly. Early observations had confirmed that the Anomaly was in motion at the exact same speed as 385571 Otrera. High-powered photography confirmed a strangely unremarkable appearance: the Anomaly was a jet-black circle within a bright white halo.

At first, the processor-analysts had been afraid that it was a black hole, its bright perimeter possibly a photonsphere of in-falling matter. Only after several days of observations of the other objects in the L4 group was it confirmed that those objects showed no signs of being gravitationally disturbed at all by the Anomaly. If it had any mass, it was negligible.

The objects of the L4 group had walked a reliable march around the Sun within a near-perfectly regular elliptical orbit since before life appeared on Earth. As such, even a slight disturbance in their march around the Sun was relatively easy to detect, like one soldier among thousands stumbling or marching off-rhythm will stand out in a battalion. The other objects of the L4 group had begun to separate, not from any propulsive force, but because the whole system had been subtly jostled by the absence of 385571 Otrera and its gravity.

This meant that 385571 Otrera had not just been destroyed. Had it exploded, or been crushed by the Anomaly somehow, its mass and therefore its gravity should remain about the same. The separation of the L4 group indicated a more dizzying puzzle: 385571 Otrera had simply vanished, together with all of its mass and gravity. The Anomaly had swallowed it up and erased it, as if 385571 Otrera had fallen through a gap in the universe, with only a bright flash of light as its farewell.

What Dr. Namur found most terrifying about the Anomaly was how it directly faced the Earth. The high-powered photography revealed, when lined up over several days, that the Anomaly not only looked down on the Earth at the time of its appearance, but it followed the Earth consistently like an eye fixated upon us. Because Neptune's L4 Lagrange does not orbit the Earth itself, this could only mean that the Anomaly was changing position, rotating at specific and irregular angles so its center always pointed directly at the Earth.

Therefore, Dr. Namur had concluded, as had many of the other neurons of the civilization-brain, that either the Anomaly was intelligent, or it was controlled by an intelligence.

There was no way to know if the Anomaly had appeared right on top of 385571 Otrera, or if the Anomaly had overtaken and consumed the object after some longer predatory advance. 385571 Otrera may have slid into the Anomaly from the side. Why that particular object, at that particular time, was unknowable based on the existing data.

Further examination of the light released by the annihilation of 385571 Otrera had revealed that it wasn't just visible light that had been released when the Anomaly consumed it. The entire electromagnetic spectrum, from gamma rays to radio waves, had lit up around 385571 Otrera like a set of wind chimes all ringing together from the same gust of wind. The collision of the Anomaly with 385571 Otrera had been loud, violent, bright, and hot.

#

Dr. Namur's train pulled into the Staples Mill Road station in Richmond late in the afternoon. He had spent the entire ride reading and re-reading the briefing materials, which had been supplied to him by the Department of Defense on a tablet that had no internet connectivity, no SIM card, and a polarized screen that would be impossible to photograph with a phone or a camera. The Anomaly briefing materials were the only files on the tablet. It didn't even have a standard operating system, just a primitive-looking command prompt line he had to use to open each of the files individually.

Such protocols served the function of protein compartmentalization in the brain. Certain proteins designed to work only with specific types of neurons are vital to life and health, but those same proteins, when improperly distributed to the wrong parts of the brain, might cause prion diseases – madness, painful death.

Dr. Namur was a processor-analyst in civilization's brain. The Anomaly briefing materials were part of his job.

To anyone else in civilization not having a specific and immediate use for them, they might lead to madness, painful death. He was, therefore, faithful to his orders to rub the tablet several times with a small, dense magnet that had also been giving to him by the Department of Defense, before even getting off the train.

He drove home in silence to the empty Richmond house. He undressed and showered while dinner defrosted. After eating, he spent the waning half-hour or so of dusk watching the fireflies from his back patio. Dr. Namur liked fireflies. He admired them; where humans spent an enormous percentage of their time and calories on seduction, the fireflies were able to resolve the matter with a flash of bioluminescence. Pheromones, mating dances, traumatic insemination, every other strategy that life had tried was simply too expensive for what the fireflies knew should be as effortless as admiring the twinkling of starlight.

The bees were already asleep for the evening, save for a few stragglers. Namur watched them lazing about below the treeline in the dying embers before nightfall. He missed the bees while they slept.

"Bizzybees! Bizzybees!" had been his terminology for them as a young child. He remembered wandering through the sprawling scrubland behind his parents' house as a child, pointing them out wherever he saw them. "Bizzybees!" He had loved the bees, the way they reflexively fed the world, like cells themselves conveying nutrition from place to place to place, the circulatory system of the chlorophyllics.

He had found ways to take the bees with him. He had purchased a smaller, more rural house as a getaway shortly after gaining his first academic employment. The rural Blackstone house had come with enough land for him to cultivate the cultivators. A dozen squat, white beekeeping stations poked up out of the unbothered grasses that fuzzed over the property. The bizzybees spent their days leaping between the tall grasses and piling wildflowers that had overtaken the previous owner's neatly-plowed fields. Blackstone, Virginia, with its sturdy metal-roofed ranch houses, was a good place to leave mostly alone, leave it to the weeds and bugs, let it grow with the ground.

The previous owner had tried a hand at tobacco but settled on wheat. Namur had let it die, doing nothing to the wheat at all except to leave it in the hands of the grass and the flowers. Now the bees had the flowers, Namur had the bees, and the detrivores had all the rest.

He added some honey to his evening tea and lay down, failing an attempt not to think. He tried not to think about his early studies in entomology, from whence to biology, from whence to an advanced degree in exobiology. He'd gotten the advanced degree thinking it would serve as pure window-dressing for a career in academic biology.

The specific thing about which he tried not to think was that the sole reason that the reflex-system and analysis-systems of civilization had agreed to disclose the Anomaly to him was that he was the closest human to Brookhaven with that advanced exobiology degree.

Horrifying, he thought, to ever consider such expertise to be important to the reflex-system. He drifted off, and had a nightmare about trudging through honey, sinking deeper into it with every step, struggling towards some distant light while suctioned ankle-deep then knee-deep and higher still into sweet sludge.

#

Several satellites had been retasked to cast a continuous gaze upon the Anomaly. While the reflex-system's asteroid deflectors would arrive in only a couple of weeks, no dedicated probe would even be ready for launch for months. It fell to the asteroid deflectors to serve as greeters, messengers, protectors, probes, and relay stations.

Dr. Namur did not immediately understand what his job was. His first meeting at Brookhaven had been almost non-verbal. He had been provided with the Anomaly briefing materials at about the same time he was told that he had been conscripted into the armed forces. He was instructed to take a sabbatical from the University of Virginia, then given a contract that multiplied his pay by ten and reduced his communication with the outside world to zero. After being told that he'd been drafted, gently compelled to execute several documents related to confidentiality which were themselves redundant in light of national security laws, he was sent on his way with nothing but the air-gapped tablet. They hadn't even given him hard copies of his contracts.

He never returned to Brookhaven. In the morning, a black car with tinted windows, which were illegal in Virginia, took him out of Richmond.

"Leave your phone or they'll arrest you. I'm taking you to the meeting site," was all the driver told him. Dr. Namur looked out the window for the entire drive. He watched gray turn to green as Richmond became Zion, then back to gray as Zion became Charlottesville, then gray to yellow then to a low-albedo white as Charlottesville became Staunton. He didn't know the area well but he knew its shape: primary producers supplied by small towns, chloroplasts or basic protein synthesis commencing the Krebs cycle of civilization with wheat and rain, sunlight, dollars, and labor. The plants of rural Virginia were different only in scale, not type, from the people, Dr. Namur included.

The black car pulled into the lot of the old Jet Weld building. Dr. Namur was unsurprised to see a dense perimeter of men with rifles ringing the facility. The shadow of a silent helicopter passed over him when he got out of the car. The helicopter served the function of a myelin sheath or the blood-brain barrier, a structure designed to protect the brain of civilization from the rest of its body and vice versa, having the same purpose and function as the confidentiality agreements he'd been made to sign.

He soon saw that, while the old Jet Weld building had been allowed to fall into a state of deliberate disrepair such that it looked like just another artifact of the desolation of rural America when viewed from its dilapidated exterior, its interior was jarringly modernized and bustling with both military uniforms and civilian-garbed scientific personnel. Considered as a design philosophy, he found the camouflage remarkably effective. Considered as an organism, Dr. Namur realized that this dense nodule of muscles and nerves, disguised by myelin, hidden within a rural plane of low-intensity primary production, resembled a malignancy more than an organ.

The driver did not follow him out of the car into the funnel of soldiers, rifles diagonal across their chests, then through a security gate and down several staircases to what could not possibly have been the original depths of the Jet Weld building. By his count, Dr. Namur was at least five stories underground. No one attempted to explain why he had been brought down by the stairs when an elevator audibly whirred nearby; he could see the elevator doors just past the landing threshold of each set of stairs.

The lowest level of the Jet Weld facility felt almost primitive to Dr. Namur. He would have expected to see at least a server bank, consoles, modern scientific equipment. On the assumption that the Jet Weld facility's purpose was to study the Anomaly, it should at least have a dedicated laser transmitter, but the top of the old building had looked like the same rusted, exposed steel he'd expect to see in any neglected industrial plat. The building overflowed with rust, from the exterior to the floors of the basement. The rust wove a continuous irregular patchwork like the mottled spiderweb arrangement of a bad throat infection, or like the grasses and wildflowers that had devoured the grounds around his Blackstone house.

There were few lab coats and no one even carried tablets. The room into which he was escorted had been clearly repurposed from a kitchen into a conference room, complete with exhaust boots and pipe fittings still intact on the walls around four long dining tables that had been pushed together in an uneven rectangle. Cheap-looking folding chairs were packed tightly around it, each occupied by a serious-looking person in one kind of uniform or another: military, suit-and-tie, some medical or engineering attire with baggy pants that had too many pockets, others the shabby-chic of academics. At least two dozen in all, packed too tightly into the small, sparse little room, like an over-booked AA meeting.

He recognized none of the faces. Given that his own field was so small, he would have expected that, had any other exobiologists of note been present, he would not only have recognized them immediately, he would likely know any such people on a first-name basis. It occurred to Dr.

Namur that there ought to be few occasions in which only a single exobiologist would be a good idea for such a meeting. The optimal number of exobiologists to have present ought to be either none, or all of them.

Almost as absurd as the apparent lack of exobiology expertise was the apparent abundance of military uniforms. The guards made sense to Dr. Namur. As the myelin sheaths of civilization, ample protection from interference passing either to or from the processing-nodes and corpuscular systems seemed sensible, for all the obvious reasons. But, to have high-level military personnel present conjured the absurd suggestion that the decision-makers considered force to be even a prospective, potential response to any situation such as this. A civilization that could create something like the Anomaly surely had as much to fear from 22nd-century humanity as 22nd-century humanity had to fear from oceanic amoebas.

Dr. Namur was brought to the table, where he quietly took a seat. He occupied the only open chair, telling him that he was the last of a full slate to arrive. Quiet, directionless conversation around the room told him that the meeting had not yet formally begun. He had received no itinerary, and there were no introductions. He didn't even have a name-tag. Only those present in military uniforms were identifiable, by the names on their lapels. He recognized none of those names either; neither the Brookhaven staff, nor anyone high enough in the military chain of command to be household names or at least politically important, were present.

"Why are you smiling?"

The older woman who had leaned over to speak to Dr. Namur kept her voice low. Her apparent inclination to keep polite conversation inaudible to the other attendees struck Dr. Namur as just another layer of myelin. The emerging model in Dr. Namur's head of the Anomaly project as a tessellated stack of well-insulated corpuscles within other, also well-insulated corpuscles, a strange tangle of incompatible fibers from systems nervous, adrenal, muscular, and reflective-processor, worried him. It felt increasingly tumorous the more he considered it.

"Names," replied Dr. Namur, gesturing with a horizontal swipe of one finger raised barely above the lip of the table, like a periscope. He hadn't realized he'd been smiling.

"I'd ask who you are, but apparently we're all nobodies." She inclined her head a few degrees to the side, and then a few degrees vertically, as if inspecting a mysterious object in the distance, when she began to playfully identify the other attendees by the ranks indicated by their lapels with names like "Lieutenant Nobody. *First* Lieutenant Nobody." She stopped and squinted at the person seated at the head of the table. "Captain… Nobody," she whispered, as if sharing a great mystery.

"Doctor Nobody. Nice to meet you." Namur extended a hand, but the room was called to order before she had the chance to humor him. She returned to her original sitting position and adopted an American Gothic scowl when the uniformed man she'd identified as First Lieutenant Nobody at the opposite end of the table rose and began speaking.

Dr. Namur was pleased that she had been able to instantly compute his meaning from a single word: "Names." Myelin is for improving electrical conductivity, in addition to protecting sensitive tissues from protein contamination or biochemical spillover, after all. Perhaps the Jet Weld project could lead to useful neural patterns after all.

The uniformed First Lieutenant began. His remarks felt prepared; Namur found it ominous that the military seemed to have an itinerary and he didn't. "You have all been briefed on what we are calling the Anomaly. Some of you do not know that our response is already underway." A wall behind the man speaking dissolved into a map of the solar system and zoomed in on the trans-Uranic orbital region. Two small illuminated objects projected purple lines towards a larger glowing circle that was clearly meant to be the Anomaly. "Asteroid deflectors, equipped with the standard load-out of fusion bombs and focused microwave emitters, have been reassigned from their original tasks, to intercept the Anomaly."

"'Intercept?'" mouthed the woman next to Dr. Namur, loudly enough for others to hear.

"Yes, Professor Nelson. The decision was made two days ago."

"Recall them!"

Dr. Namur puzzled over the ability of this civilian scientist next to him to deign to give instructions. His own default position, now as it had been for much of his life, was to sit quietly until summoned or prompted.

"It can't be done." This response came from another man, this one in the distinctive lighter blue uniform of the planetary defense forces. This was the one branch of the United States military that was permitted to fully integrate with other nations and with international forces. His lapels indicated the rank of Captain. A name was sewn into his breast pocket: Captain J. Ogden. "These are the two deflectors that were closest to the Anomaly. We had one burn all of its fuel for maximum acceleration. The other has burned half its fuel to accelerate, and will need the rest to decelerate in time to reach a stable parking orbit within visual range of the Anomaly."

Dr. Namur understood the reflex. Like swatting a stinging wasp, the hand that swats often reacts faster than the eyes that find the wasp. This was the incorrect reflex – the Anomaly was not a wasp – but Dr. Namur understood the reasoning. Civilization was adapted for its immediate environment. It dawned on him that his reason for being there was to determine what sort of new selective pressure the Anomaly represented: environmental change? Invasive species?

One of the civilian scientists quickly exchanged a whisper with Captain Ogden, then leaned forwards over the table to draw the others' attention. "The first deflector is being sent at maximum speed to get us at least some information as quickly as possible. We intend the second deflector to serve as a proper probe. It will give us a visual feed, and it has all of the same spectrometry and chromatography equipment you'd find on an asteroid prospector, plus top-of-the-line astrometrics, range-finding, and mass analysis."

The screen behind Captain Ogden changed again, now zooming in closer to the faster-moving of the two asteroid deflectors. The small, roughly diamond-shaped spacecraft rotated on the screen to an undercarriage view, and red outlines highlighted its armament.

Captain Ogden continued. By how the civilian scientist had seemingly reported to him, Dr. Namur began to wonder if Ogden was the military senior in the room. "Each deflector carries a payload of fusion bombs. They're intended for detonation on the surface of asteroids to destroy them, or at least steer them out of dangerous trajectories. They're the standard deuterium-tritium fast-fission style, with yields in the 200-terajoule range." Captain Ogden turned to touch the screen, dragging his index finger along a blue line connecting the image of the deflector to the representation of the Anomaly. "The first deflector will pass very close to the Anomaly. Its maneuvering thrusters are precise enough to let us set its interception range very close, or even to have it make direct contact with the Anomaly."

This led to another startled flurry of adrenal activity around the table. Dr. Namur contributed nothing to the ensuing conversation about whether or not the first deflector should fly past the Anomaly, or fly through it. The Anomaly was a few hundred meters in diameter; it wasn't a question of whether or not the maneuver could be accomplished.

"Alternatively, we *could* detonate the fusion bombs."

Dr. Namur was surprised to hear that suggestion come from one of the civilians. An older man, who spoke with a dense Balkan accent, offered the suggestion loudly enough to quiet the others.

That man rose, and continued speaking. "Because this entire ludicrous little cavalcade was badly organized by people who crave secrecy over the kind of collaborative exchange required of any good science, none of you know me yet. Not even the other scientists know me. My name is Petrovic. I am an obscure and unremarkable academic. The sole reason I am here is because I am the only astronomer Captain Ogden could find through a quick internet search who had published a paper on 385571 Otrera's orbital dynamics. That paper was uninteresting, and it has never been cited. As I have no career of note at risk and no notoriety to lose, I may be direct. We should detonate the fusion bomb upon interception of the Anomaly, preferable directly upon or inside it, and we should do so *just to see what happens*." He rapped a knuckle against the table to emphasize each of his concluding words.

Voltage potential charged.

The only thing that surprised Dr. Namur more than Petrovic's pronouncement was that he was compelled, in the almost involuntary fashion of glossolalia, to murmur a "hear, hear" – his first contribution to the meeting louder than a whisper.

Voltage potential released.

"Dr. Namur." An angular, wiry woman in an Air Force uniform who, when she stood to address the room, let everyone see that she wore a sidearm on her hip, diverted everyone's attention away from Petrovic and onto Dr. Namur with a slicing gesture of her palm. It took Namur a moment to realize that this gesture was intended to summon him to stand up. "I am merely annoyed to hear this opinion from," she swept the same hand back towards Petrovic, "this sad fellow here. He strikes me as constitutionally gloomy. I wonder which Tolstoy novel we drafted him from. But to hear some kind of approval for this idea from our only *bona fide* alien expert is, frankly, unsettling. Please, elaborate."

Voltage potentials charged and released, charged and released, inside Dr. Namur, with terrific random. Millions and millions of voltage potentials and whole thoughts and decisions bubbled in and out of existence in the seconds it took him to rise. The axles of civilization wheeled around the Jet Weld building, Dr. Namur realized, and he did not like it. The outsized power of these few people, in this small place, to compress and direct all of the thoughts, goals, dreams, motives, and powers of civilization in a single direction, had the function and likeness of a seizure, or a bubbling-over of the DRD2 receptor as in a major psychotic episode.

Shall we all go insane together, then?

He restrained himself from saying this thought aloud. Myelin sheaths within myelin sheaths.

"Ah, yes, I am Dr. Aram Namur. I… hm. I was brought here by Brookhaven, they reached out to me first. Before that, the University of Virginia... never mind my CV. I am here, and you are correct about my credentials, my areas of study. I am a biologist by trade. That is the subject I teach. But, I hold an advanced degree in astrobiology, which I use for more or less nothing except an elective seminar I teach every other semester." He held his palms out as if to apologize or shrug, and was relieved to see smiles and chuckles around the table.

A voltage potential defused *in situ*, no-action signal, false-alarm signal.

"The detonation of the bombs aboard the deflector would teach us about the Anomaly. Light scattering through it will enable us to analyze it chromatographically," he continued.

"We can shine the deflector's docking lights on it for that!" protested the woman named Nelson, still sitting next to Dr. Namur's seat. "There's no need to destroy the thing in the process!"

Dr. Namur took his seat again so he could speak to her directly. He was pleased that all of the eyes in the room followed him. "Whatever the Anomaly is, the fusion bomb will not destroy it. It consumed a large trans-Neptunian object, and has apparently obviated its mass entirely. How it did this, I do not know. It must have vaporized Otrera so thoroughly that its mass has been scattered into particulate dust too fine to see at a distance, even as a halo or a cloud. It also appeared suddenly, and it is looking right at us. It is fantastically advanced technology. I am beyond the point of suspecting that it is of an extra-solar intelligence. It is adjusting its angle to follow us, watchfully, thoughtfully. And it appeared out of nowhere, indicating a type or a method of transportation completely unknown to our physics. We cannot begin to speculate about its origin, purpose, or make."

"And how will blowing it up help with that?" Professor Nelson's tone was increasingly exasperated.

Namur diverted his eyes away from hers and turned in his seat to face the table to enunciate the conclusion he thought would be obvious by now. "The creators of the Anomaly possess technology about which we can scarcely begin to contemplate. If they are here to destroy us, they will do so and it will be effortless for them. Because the Anomaly went completely unobserved until it destroyed Otrera, it must be capable of traveling so quickly that even minor collisions with transient space dust would have damaged it far more than a fusion bomb will, meaning that the fusion bomb will not injure it in the slightest. If they are here for some other purpose, they will understand that we are conducting ordinary science, which we are."

"I disagree," Professor Nelson replied. His goodwill with her was already gone, Namur detected sourly. "Force is force. A bee is substantially less intelligent and less developed than a human, but a bee-sting will still hurt." She paused for effect, timed precisely long enough to render artificial profundity to her next words without leaving enough space to be interrupted. Dr. Namur was pleased by her ability to create and discharge a tension-potential so effortlessly. "And it will get itself swatted and its nest gassed for its trouble."

Voltage potential charged.

Dr. Namur's heartbeat briefly accelerated. From her words, he had deduced the purpose of the Anomaly. There was only one thing for him to do, or rather – nothing.

"Busy bees," he murmured.

"Doctor Namur?" That was the Air Force woman again. Namur imagined that her fingers played along the flank of her holstered sidearm for the same reason, and to the same effect, that others twirled a pencil or cracked their knuckles to keep their fingers busy. "What did you say?"

"Oh. Bizzybees, it's…."

Aram Namur's eyes settled on the screen behind Captain Ogden. In the extended blue line that flowed from the first asteroid deflector to the Anomaly, Namur saw briefly a return trajectory, then in his mind's eye the return trajectory extended in both directions at once, forming a connection measured in diopters... then a pathway, like an old dirt road overgrown on both sides with piling wildflowers open to foot traffic both ways. A neuron, two neurons, a sodium channel, a potassium channel, an axon terminal joined together by… what? What was the Anomaly's neurotransmitter?

A bee is substantially less intelligent and less developed than a human. I miss the bees.

He felt the flutter of membrane wings rising around his ankles on either side of that dirt road, the bizzybees coming up with the dawn to do as they must. The taste of honey formed in the back of his throat.

There were too many eyes – all of the eyes in the room besides his – focused on him in that lengthy silence to permit such a prolonged reverie. Worse, he immediately concluded, he would be laughed out of ever getting to play even a trivial role in the next phases of the Jet Weld project if he spoke aloud any of the objectively crazy things he now knew, with certainty, about the Anomaly.

He gestured to Captain Ogden, and spoke directly to him. "Everything will be fine." He chuckled. "Better than fine. This will be wonderful."

Dr. Namur then got up and left.

Voltage potential released.

The fact that no one tried to stop him told Dr. Namur quite a bit about the true extent of the Jet Weld project's actual authority.

The same person who had driven him to the Jet Weld building drove him back to Richmond in uninterrupted silence.

#

The night that he left the Jet Weld building, Dr. Namur had himself driven back to Richmond, and from there he drove himself to his rural Blackstone house. He packed only a toothbrush, some clothes, and several packs of instant coffee. He had decided even before leaving that it would be the Richmond house that would be let alone now. Blackstone would become a proper home.

He pulled into the Blackstone house's dirt driveway, already partially encroached-upon by tufts of green and yellow, just as the sun was setting. A second black car pulled up and parked along the narrow frontage road running perpendicular to the driveway; myelin followed him, ensuring his compliance with his confidentiality agreements and observance of national security protocols.

He walked through the front door and dropped his bag on the floor. The ancient instant coffee maker tucked among cobwebs on the kitchen counter still apparently worked, based on the way its clock blinked 12:00 12:00 12:00 12:01 12:01 12:01 12:02… while he prepared the instant coffee for brewing, but did not press BREW yet. He then tucked his pant legs into his socks, and exited through the back door.

Through waist-high grasses he strolled, calmly and quietly, eyes fixed on the nearest beekeeper's stand, hands out palms-down to either side to tickle his palms with the tips of the grasses and the petals of the wildflowers. Things bit at him here and there. He noticed and was bothered, but considered it his role. His proteins fed the field and its keepers and its pollinators. Cells from him became cells out there.

He thought of the Anomaly. He couldn't stop laughing.

He reached the beekeeper's stand. He pulled off the black faux-shingle cap and reached an un-gloved hand inside. It disturbed the bees greatly, though he had mostly shaken them off by the time he got back to the house with a palm full of dripping honeycomb. He flecked aside the last bee, dead with its stinger in his wrist, and crammed the goopy mess into a dirty mug from a cabinet. He pressed BREW and, a minute later, poured the brown sludge into the mug, swirled it briefly, sipped to taste, then drank heartily with a smile on his face.

#

Dr. Namur knew that the military people would find a way to drag him back into the Anomaly project. He assumed they'd come knocking sometime around the arrival of the first asteroid deflector. He knew this left him with little time to prepare, though he didn't know the arrival date or time with precision. Professor Nelson had already informed him, in her own way, of the final outcome to the Anomaly phenomenon, what it represented for the present and the future, for the arc of speciation among civilizations. He was suffused with a cautious vitality, finding himself the guardian of secret knowledge, annoyed as he was that nobody else in the Jet Weld project had seen so clearly as he could.

He needed two days to prepare the Blackstone house. The first day was spent driving up and down Charlottesville, exhausting the battery in his car twice. He stopped at every electronics store he knew, filling his trunk with modular circuits, updated audio equipment for his computer, a telescope, attachments for the telescope to help it to track the Anomaly and other objects in the sky, extra monitors, extra computers, jugs of water, canned food. The process felt vaguely placental to him, gathering rare nutrients with which to construct and feed a brain at Blackstone.

Namur spent the second day rigging the Blackstone house with all of this new equipment. He set out early on the third day, a travel mug full of honeyed coffee in the center console for the drive back to Richmond. While he had little professional overlap with the University of Virginia's humanities departments, he had maintained friendships across the faculty. He had tried not to sound too desperately transactional on the phone with DeWit, a junior lecturer in the economics department. Because DeWit hadn't yet earned tenure, it fell to him to teach introductory courses, which meant he would be steeped in precisely the sort of knowledge that Dr. Namur sought.

The restaurant sourced its material inputs locally. The food that it served came from places like Blackstone. The capital that it ingested, digested, and processed into service delivery by distribution to its own proteins was sourced from Richmonders like DeWit directly. Capital would cycle back out to the primary producers in places like Blackstone, restarting the Krebs cycle of civilization.

Namur and DeWit sat across from each other and caught up. News of the Anomaly had not yet reached the general public, though he knew it was only a matter of time. Amateur and civilian astronomy would take a little while longer, since the trans-Neptunian orbit was not of particular interest to the astronomy crowd the way that more distant stellar observation was, but something like the Anomaly could only go unnoticed for so long. He did not have a good feel for what its disclosure would mean for the world, or for his ability to have conversations like this one with DeWit.

"Tell me about trade." Namur had allowed several minutes of unproductive idle chatter beforehand; he was mindful of his confidentiality agreements. While paranoia was not in his nature, he took note of at least one overdressed observer, black suit, black tie, glancing up from his phone towards their table from time to time. While he knew not the instrumentality, Namur was sure that every word he exchanged with DeWit was being overlooked.

Insects participated in the conversation in their own way. They, too, were sourced locally, their homes clustered around the Chimborazo Community Garden just a block away from the restaurant. The Chimborazo bees were not like the Blackstone bees, who fed from well-prepared if ill-kept beekeeping stands that allowed them to build and arrange their civilization to its peak sustainable population. The Chimborazo bees were subject to the vicissitudes of a transient and inconsistent food supply, frequent human entry and egress, even the urban weather of more metal-dense air, shadows from tall buildings, particulate matter from street cleaning. The Chimborazo bees therefore sought food with the greater greed of heightened urgency, and sought it farther from home, with little guaranteed to them the way the Blackstone bees would always have a safe place to extrude their rich protein lattices.

A Chimborazo bee attempted to intervene upon Professor DeWit's salad, but was brushed aside.

"Trade. Well, trade is good. Could you be more specific?"

Namur tried not to make eye contact with his shadow a few tables away. "What makes trade good? Viewed as between nations, say, not between companies."

DeWit angled his tall, spindly body forwards over the table. The sleeve of his smart, light-colored jacket was tugged up by the crooking of his elbows against the table when he folded his hands together in a quintessentially professorial pose, to reveal an inexpensive watch on his wrist. "I suppose I could start by asking you how come we're ordering food from this restaurant, instead of storming the kitchen, killing the staff, and taking the food."

"The waiter alone is half my age. Twice my size, too, though maybe not yours."

DeWit laughed, gesturing dismissively. "But, even if it would work…"

"We'd get in trouble."

"...and even if you could get away with it, you'd only do something like that out of desperation. Why? Because they have food and they know how to prepare it well. They have something you want today, and they're likely to have something you want tomorrow, and the day after that, and the day after that. Laws aside, it's in your best interest to keep exchanging something they want –

money, in our case – for the things you want. If they wanted something else, like those bees you keep or something, something you're likely to have tomorrow and the day after as well, it'd be in your best interest to keep up that exchange. Using violence isn't just dangerous, it's counterproductive. It deprives you of a recurring source of something you want."

Namur nodded along. He had spent much of the drive into Richmond trying to come up with an explanation for why he was asking so many Econ 101 questions. Though, as the conversation unfolded, he was pleased to find that he had accurately prefigured that DeWit would, like so many other young lecturers, like nothing more than to talk about their chosen area of expertise for as long as possible. Confabulations may not be necessary.

A Chimborazo bee took a seat beside Namur's plate. Namur noticed but did not disturb it. He did not even try to prevent its cautious approach to the side of his plate. He watched the flutter of its membrane-wings for a moment, even while DeWit continued talking. The way its wide, flat wings flitted nervously each time its little legs tiptoed closer to his plate, as if digging a path through the air through which the bee might crawl, made Namur listen for music.

The high-pitched hiss of those wings must surely sound different to every bee. Rich music in swarms of thousands – do bees hear counterpoint?, Namur wondered. He risked another glance towards his shadow before DeWit continued.

"Another thing you'll notice," DeWit continued, "is that you know how to cook food too. You don't need the restaurant. In fact, you're good with nature. I bet that, left to your own devices, you could grow the same plants and raise the same animals you're out here spending money on at this restaurant. Why don't you? For too many reasons to count. You just have other things to do. Other things you'd rather do, other things you need to do."

"Okay, okay," Namur had to cut DeWit off. He still hadn't eaten anything. He decided that he was going to let the Chimborazo bee try it first. "That's us and the restaurant. I'm talking about nations. Civilizations."

"Same thing, different scales." DeWit produced his phone and tapped its screen a couple of times. "Look at a map of where people make coffee." DeWit showed him. "There are a lot of reasons for this. Climate mostly. Everybody drinks coffee. So, why aren't we constantly at war to seize the means of coffee production? Because it's cheaper to buy it than to conquer it. It's also cheaper to buy it than to make it. Not even Virginia's hottest, wettest summer would be a suitable climate for becoming a primary producer of coffee. The expense of tempering the environment to do so would outstrip the profitability even of coffee. Not only that, but our agricultural land is busy with other things – corn, wheat, soybeans."

"Tobacco," Namur observed.

"Tobacco! Yes, something nobody needs, but which is immensely more profitable than food. And yet, here in America, we have way more land, better access to top-rate equipment and capital for farms, an endless supply of migrant labor. Why do we still buy food? Because no matter how much we produce, and no matter how good we are at it, there's still something else we can have by trade. Even if we utterly cornered the coffee market, the coffee-producing places would switch to some other suitable crop, and then we'd buy that. *The reason we trade for things is because there are things to trade for*. Our need for it is immaterial. Our ability to produce it for ourselves is immaterial. We have something they want, they have something we want, and swapping them is the surest, most efficient path to having it. The fact that we *both* benefit from it is purely incidental, but advantageous to each of us."

Namur watched the Chimborazo bee experimentally tap at a piece of lettuce before taking flight again. He ate quietly for a moment. "But lets suppose," and at this point, his shadow a few tables away was clearly listening. Though sunglasses shielded his eyes, Namur had no doubt that he was being watched – or stared down. "For argument's sake, that the other country has nothing to offer in trade. No industry or agriculture."

DeWit gestured to either side, as if to somehow demonstrate the existence of the Commonwealth of Virginia. "You still find something to trade. Conquest is simply too expensive. Even when it doesn't stop civilization entirely, it slows it down. Contrary to common opinion, our wars with the indigenous peoples of the Americas were neither inevitable nor beneficial. Had we engaged in fulsome trade with them, we'd have the same country with richer Native Americans in it. Likewise for slavery in the south. By robbing millions of people of wages, by slowing the need for labor-saving mechanization because the labor was free, the American South hobbled itself economically for generations. Look at any GDP heatmap of the South and the North. Even now, almost three hundred years after the Civil War, the economic disparity remains uncured. Trading money for labor is better than stealing it. Paid labor is better for everyone, including the ones paying for it."

"Okay, but still-" Namur felt himself approaching the edge of a line the crossing of which would imperil his freedom or his life, but considered both immaterial at the moment, "-those societies did have things to offer in trade, even if we declined it. Land, labor, these are all things we might want to buy. But just suppose, whether we want to trade with them or not, the other nation truly has nothing we might want to buy. Pretend their religion forbids them from selling labor or land. Do whatever you need to do to pretend along with me. The other nation has nothing for sale. Closed for business."

After tapping his phone a couple more times, DeWit turned it around to show a map with a few small countries highlighted in red. "Sanctioned countries. Countries it's illegal to trade with. What do we do with them?" He made a helpless gesture with the upturned palm of the other hand. "Nothing. We never invaded North Korea or Khorasan or any of the other places that have disappeared themselves from the market. They're economic dead-zones. We have enough history to know that conquest is an inefficient tool for economic expansion."

"Not always. Europe grew up on colonies."

DeWit seemed suddenly pleased with himself. "Colonies were net losers for colonial empires for generations. They're a massive investment. When they do eventually pay off, it's mainly because of the trade you get from them. Britain made more from trade with India in the decade after its independence than in the century before. If you were proposing it as a rational economic undertaking, the sole argument you'd have in favor of colonization is whether or not it cultivates a future trade partner."

Cultivates. Namur smiled. The Chimborazo bee hovered briefly around his face, perhaps confusing the gold-colored temple tip of his glasses for a flower. The sound of its pounding wings formed a lilting major chord two hundred times a second.

"Thank you, Mr. DeWit." He raised his glass in a toast, apologetically, as if having consumed something of DeWit's for himself without exchange. When DeWit drank from his cup, Namur turned his head ever so slightly to give the same gesture to his shadow. They ate and drank over unrelated social chatter for the rest of the meal. The Chimborozo bee left with flecks of salt and seasoning on its legs and antennae.

#

Not only did Namur not know how fast the first deflector was traveling towards the Anomaly, it had taken him only the glance at the deflector's schematics he had gotten at the Jet Weld meeting to realize that it would be impossible for him to deduce it from information available to him. There was no way to know how much fuel the deflector was carrying when it was ordered to a full acceleration burn, nor was there any way to know exactly when it had been ordered to do so.

All of the equipment he had purchased and installed around the Blackstone house's living room proved unhelpful in this regard. He couldn't even get a fix on the asteroid deflectors without knowing their original positions. The only way to know such things would be to resume communications with the various defense agencies. As this was impossible, he resigned himself to waiting for a phone call or a knock on the door.

He was, however, able to pinpoint the Anomaly itself after just a few minutes of scanning. This alarmed him. He didn't even need to know 385571 Otrera's original position. Instructing the telescope he had set up in the back yard to search Neptune's leading and trailing Lagrangians for bright lights was all it took. Unless the military found a way to throw a tarp over the entire Neptunian orbital radius, amateur astronomers would soon have word out about an eye in the sky.

The energy transfer was one-way: hormonal transfer from the civilization-brain to him could not be returned. He could but dissipate this energy throughout the body, but if he were to dissipate it too quickly or improperly, he could be imprisoned or worse over violations of confidentiality, like the immune system attacking a hematoma.

His conversation with DeWitt had pushed the line. He knew that had he so much as tried to leave the Blackstone house with a copy of the deflector's schematics, either on his phone or a physical copy, they would have found a way to stop him. He was just as confident that all of his communications were being monitored, and conducted himself under the assumption that his home had been bugged.

Even basic internet research on things like the distance to Neptune felt risky. A sufficiently clever algorithmic tracker or AI pattern-matching tool might have been able to connect his browser cookies into a coherent story. But, he had to take the chance.

Distance to Neptune: four light hours. Difference in orbital radius between Neptune and 385571 Otrera: negligible. Price of a precision radio transmitter: prohibitive. So much for that. He would not be able to send messages of his own to the Anomaly.

In those days of preparation, he deliberately disconnected as much of the internet as he could from the Blackstone house. He sent and received no emails or text messages. He'd considered this a form of cautionary prophylaxis against accidentally trespassing upon his confidentiality obligations.

His spam filter blocked the Massachusetts area code that finally tried to call him. It was only after four or five different numbers from that same area code tried to call him that Dr. Namur responded, the way the body makes an itch worse by giving into its nervous transmission for a scratch.

"You're up to something."

That was Professor Nelson on the other end. She must have come from M.I.T. or Harvard, one of those sorts of places. It occurred to Dr. Namur that he hadn't even bothered to learn her field of expertise. Engineering? The sciences? By the way she had spoken to the Jet Weld team, it might have been business management or psychology.

"I've been conscripted," she continued, in her terse, almost stunted way, "to ask you back before they drag you back." Efficient, angry, and he knew that she meant she'd been selected to try to re-open communication with him because she was simply stronger than him in the ways that mattered. "They know that you figured something out. They need to know what it is, but they can't pay you any more for it. Something about the budget allocation becoming public." She paused here and there, inviting Namur to speak, but he didn't. "Okay, turn on the news."

It had been several days since he had checked any feeds. He'd long ago deactivated notifications related to the news on his phone, seeing no need to ingest that sort of neurotoxin voluntarily. She waited in silence, listening to his footsteps on the smooth vinyl floor as he searched up and down the Blackstone house until he found an actual television. He didn't want to retask any of his computer screens for the purpose, having dedicated all of his new equipment to processor-synthesis roles regarding the Anomaly. The dusty flatscreen he eventually found was a simple plug-and-play, and once plugged, the news it began to play unnerved him without surprising him.

The secret was out. It took only a few clicks through the available channels, scanning the subtitles under the various talking heads, to realize that the public now knew that the Anomaly existed, but nothing of its nature or purpose. Same as the Jet Weld group. Same as the military. Same, so far as Dr. Namur new, as everyone on Earth but him.

Dr. Namur understood the bees, and he understood trade. The only thing he didn't know was what the Anomaly-builders had to offer him.

"When will the first deflector arrive?" Namur finally asked.

"Come back to Jet Weld and I'll tell you."

"Okay."

Dr. Namur was not surprised to see the same dark car pulling into the driveway less than an hour later. He'd had just enough time to have another mug of honeycomb sludge, his hands glowing with bright little bee-sting marks.

#

His return to Jet Weld was met with performative anger. He was searched upon arrival and again at the bottom of the stairs. He noticed that, this time, the elevator was in more or less constant use, with uniformed soldiers rolling hand-carts filled with electronics to seemingly every floor of the building. It was being converted into a proper command center. From what he could gather from the banks of monitors now running across seemingly every square foot of walls not occupied by doors or windows, the

Jet Weld building was being turned into a kind of passive super-processor, monitoring and synthesizing all of the civilian analysis being conducted independently around the world. Rumor, speculation, astronomy, radiological analysis, from the insane to the mundane, Jet Weld was building something coherent from everything.

Becoming a true brain, Namur thought, though what thoughts it would produce remained to be seen. Today, he assumed, he would see several.

He also noticed that the Jet Weld building had been fortified. Even aerial batteries and banks of anti-drone lasers ringed the catwalks of the old building. Rows of sandbag fortifications formed a maze of curves up the long access road to the hangar-sized main doors.

The main room of the bottom floor into which he was escorted, where he was searched for a third time at the entrance to the conference room, had also been transformed. His first day in Jet Weld had felt like a Somethings-Anonymous meeting in the basement of a church, with its cheap long tables and folding chairs. Now, several walls had been taken out, so that the lowest level of the Jet Weld building was mostly a large open space ringed with concentric banks of computers, with a single wall-length conference room segregated to one side by a narrow single door and black-fogged glass walls. Through the door he saw Professor Nelson, Captain Ogden, and several others.

"Glad you could join us," Ogden greeted him with ill-concealed annoyance.

Namur took a seat, with Professor Nelson opposite him across the long, narrow black conference table that occupied most of the room. None of the other military people seemed particularly interested in his return.

"The first deflector is going to reach the Anomaly tonight." Ogden tapped a touchscreen on the table, which raised a map on one of the wall screens. "Four hours later, we will know what happened when its return signal reaches the Earth. There have been lots of… interesting theories about what might happen going around. We are under enormous pressure to divert and recall both deflectors, or to order the first one to detonate immediately. I know that some in this room share some of these opinions…"

A dyspeptic growl surged from various corners of the table, like the acceleration of the heartbeat under an anxious thought. Provocation by nothing at all.

"We don't know what it is! Aliens? Horseshit. We're driving society insane and wasting two asteroid deflectors for nothing." By his uniform, Dr. Namur took him to also be Air Force. "Our careers will be ruined when the photography shows that this whole thing is just… dust or something, a trick of the light in the remains of Otrera after a freak collision with some other rock out there. Does anyone want to guess what the combined budgetary outlay of the Jet Weld renovations has been?"

"It's much worse than that." She was smartly-dressed, all in black under a dark green Army jacket, with a sidearm that protruded over the edge of the table when she leaned forwards. She steepled her fingers and looked around the table; Namur counted the pauses in the steady horizontal scan of her eyes around the room, so as to count how many people supported whatever she was about to say. "We *do* know that it is extra-terrestrial in design. There is no other explanation for its apparent lock on the Earth. For all we know, these creatures send this thing out to every planet they find within the habitable zone of its star, and programmed it to destroy such worlds at the first sign of intelligence."

Professor Nelson scoffed. "Why wait? Captain – is that your rank? I think that's what your epaulets are supposed to mean." She did not wait for a reply. "The Anomaly appeared from nowhere and eliminated Otrera. We have enough data already to know that there's no gravitational excess. Otrera wasn't just destroyed, the mass, the energy that makes it up is entirely gone. This is impossible, and they made it happen. Any species with that kind of technology would have no reason to start with Otrera. Destroy prospective rivals, or don't."

Namur had reclined back in his chair. He closed his eyes, which he hoped would give others the impression that he was thinking intently. He was simply tired, the expensive ergonomic upgrade from the prior visit's cheap folding chairs was comfortable, and the room was warm. He pictured a web beginning with petroleum extraction in one hemisphere, the production of felt fiber in another, combining to make the plastic parts and the snug armrests of the chair. It all converged upon him like water coursing down a gutter and fertilizing the lichens and the grass and the mold that would eat Blackstone and pull it into the ground some day.

Professor Nelson and the woman in black, an Army intelligence professional with the improbable name of Cello stitched onto her jacket pocket, argued uselessly. They together produced a voltage potential that did not discharge at all, but formed a separate thought entirely in the form of Captain J. Ogden's next words.

"The second deflector is already decelerating. It will take four days longer to reach the Anomaly. At this time, its instructions are to use the last of its fuel to assume an orbit around the Sun at nearly the same distance as Otrera, to maintain a continuous distance from it of just a few kilometers. However, if the first deflector meets any trouble at all, the second deflector will instead use the last of its fuel to approach the Anomaly and detonate. The entire payload detonating at once can generate an 800-terajoule blast. In the vacuum of space, without air or dirt or debris to turn into shrapnel, such blasts are only effective as weapons in direct contact, or nearly so."

While he spoke, a large black screen behind him had formed the image of a diagram of both maneuvers, the plans displayed side-by-side. Namur noticed that the images were far more detailed now, reflecting the steadily better and better equipment that Jet Weld had consumed, assimilated, through its steel walls in its development towards a unique, standalone brain.

"What kind of diagnostic information will we get from the deflector? After it passes through the Anomaly, I mean." These were the first words that Dr. Namur had spoken since his return to Jet Weld.

"The deflector's telemetry is very thorough. It is designed to be able to understand the composition of asteroids it encounters in an instant, creating thorough compositional profiles in the tiny interval between contacting the surface of an asteroid and detonating," explained one of the few labcoat-clads in the room. A genuine engineer, a genuine protein-synthesizer, trapped in an organelle of reaction. His lapel read *Lusac.*

Dr. Namur held out his upturned palms, apologetically. "Yes, I understand. I meant internal diagnostics. How much will we be able to know about the physical state of the deflector itself once it has passed through?"

"Nothing," Professor Nelson interjected. She tapped the table impatiently. "The Anomaly is a wormhole. Artificially constructed or not, this is the only explanation for how Otrera's mass could disappear without traveling gradually away. The deflector will go to wherever Otrera has gone. We'll never hear from it again, mark my words."

Lusac took a moment before continuing, seemingly afraid of interrupting any of the louder personalities in the room. "Erm, barring its disappearance, we'll know quite a bit. The deflectors broadcast a robust diagnostic profile at all times. Because it takes so long to repair or replace them, we like to know right away if one of them is having a problem."

Among Lusac, Nelson, Ogden, Cello, and all the other, bigger personalities in the room, military and civilian, Namur was surprised to hear the imminent question come first from quiet, droopy Petrovic, whose entire personality radiated a dispiriting air.

"Why ever do you ask, Dr. Namur?" Namur took Petrovic's frown-shaped smile to mean, 'Not that I care, but....' "What do you hope to gain from internal diagnostics of the deflector that you would not gain from its telemetry?" Petrovic tapped the side of his lumpy, gray-maned skull. "And why do I suspect you'll keep the truth locked up from us?"

Namur had considered his possible responses to such a question well in advance. As a student of xenobiology, he was acutely aware that his limited usefulness would be immediately exhausted the moment he was believed to be crazy or a fantasist, and that this had to be balanced against the fact that, in principle, the only true purpose of a xenobiologist is to be something of a fantasist in the first place.

The prefix xeno- before the name of any profession would ordinarily immediately cause a conversational counterpart to ask something about UFOs or little green men, or to recite some pet theory about lights in the sky or government cover-ups.

Never mind that the entire Jet Weld cabal was, in and of itself, a badly failed government cover-up.

Namur resumed pretending to be thinking. He knew that he couldn't get away with silence or with something dismissive along the lines of 'just curious.' He had decided beforehand to simply tell the truth, and was fortunate to be able to deliver it as if to Petrovic directly and privately. "Mr. Petrovic, you know well the risks of being perceived as inconsequential in a room such as this, as well as the rewards of having little to lose. *You* have little to lose in the sense of having little at stake. *I* have little to lose in the sense of having places I would rather be than at this table. I have left before, after all.

"The simple fact is that I have a great deal of confidence in a facially absurd hypothesis about what is going to happen. If I recite it in detail, I will be presumed to be crazy. In such an event I will get to leave but I will not be permitted to return, which I might like to do after all of this has shaken out."

Namur ignored a scoff shared between Nelson and Cello.

"What I will say is this. The internal telemetry of the deflector will show that something is missing from it – a component, some part of its structure. Something will then emerge from the Anomaly, almost immediately, and we will need the second deflector to examine exactly what it is that emerges. The third thing that we should send to the Anomaly should be a great big wad of whatever material or substance goes missing from the first deflector, as big as we can make it, as fast as we can get it there."

The ensuing silence was not long-lived. It was Petrovic's laughter, followed by Professor Nelson's, that did it. Namur was pleased at first, perceiving that they had seemingly joined him in having solved the riddle.

Alas, Professor Nelson's reply made it clear that she hadn't fully unpacked it yet. He realized that he couldn't be sure who from the Jet Weld team would have been told about his lunch with DeWit. "And if the entire deflector disappears, we should just keep sending… more deflectors? In your estimation?"

"Yes," Namur replied calmly. "In that case, we should send more deflectors. In fact, we should, in such a circumstance, convert the entire industrial excess of the planet, and the orbital shipyards, and the Lunar facilities, and Mars, to the production of asteroid deflectors. We should modulate their designs and swap different components and even materials into future generations of asteroid deflectors, to determine if we get different results from the Anomaly."

To his surprise, it was Lusac, the engineer who seemed to be the only pure technician in the group, who spoke up before Professor Nelson could. "Dr. Namur, if I take your meaning, you are *not* saying that we should do so because so many deflectors would be needed to repel some kind of… alien invasion."

This charged voltage potentials around the room. The reflex-systems were stirring, and had to be defused.

"Absolutely. Professor Nelson is entirely correct that there is no chance at all that the Anomaly is here to hurt us. A species with such engineering abilities, with any motivation at all to hurt us, would not have started with

Otrera. They alerted us to their presence, and are awaiting our reply. That," he pointed at the monitor on which the flight paths of the deflectors were displayed, "is our reply, and it is an adequate one. In short," he nodded to Captain Ogden, who was visibly not amused, "I endorse the present plan, subject only to the limitation that we should not interpret damage to, or disability of, the first deflector as a hostile action. You will see. The deflector will pass through the Anomaly, and then something will emerge. I have already given you the proper course of action to follow. I am only useful to the next phase if I do not elaborate further."

"This is horseshit!" declaimed Cello. "I'm not playing riddles with the bug doctor. Nobody says 'alien invasion' in this room without making their brains transparent to all of us, right fucking quick. If you know something, that's national security information. If you're planning something, those are national security plans. If you're guessing something, that's a *preliminary* national security plan." It was pure bluster and outrage up until the moment the flank of her index finger caressed the holster of her sidearm. Everyone in the room noticed this, and the temperature seemed to drop ten degrees at once. Up until that one gesture, she might even have been kidding, certainly exaggerating at least. "You," pointing to Namur, "or you," then to Lusac, "out with it, or you can go back to your friend in the economics department and have him explain the Prisoner's Dilemma to you."

Namur's eyes flew horizontally around the room. This may have registered as a nervous look, which was helpful to his position. In reality, he was looking to see who seemed surprised or confused by this remark about the economics department, and who didn't. Ogden knew.

Nobody else did, though others may simply have been better-practiced at manually restraining their facial expressions.

Inconsistent voltage potentials, potentials with uneven pathways for release, around the table. Recipe for stroke. Or mental illness.

Civilization may go mad, or begin going far madder, within the next thirty seconds.

He hadn't long to let the wheels turn. Lusac would be speaking up soon.

"Leave Lusac out of this." Namur decided that anger was the appropriate tone for a masking reply. "He knows as well as anyone that we're not fighting the aliens' military. Winning or losing is irrelevant. If they were here to fight, that would already be obvious. They aren't. They're therefore here for something else. Going to meet them with the deflector is our version of communicating with them. They knew we were intelligent before they arrived – obviously, that's why they sent the Anomaly. Our first message to them is fundamentally defensive in nature. They'll recognize an asteroid deflector when they see one; assuming that physics works the same everywhere, microwaves and fusion bombs are logical asteroid deflectors. Bombs for deflection, microwaves to sublimate frozen elements on the surface of asteroids to change their trajectories with the resulting steam ejections. They'll send some message in reply indicating their understanding of our message, and we'll be…" he separated, and clapped his hands together again, "off to the races, so to speak."

If this lengthy *non sequitur* held, civilization might endure indefinitely into the future. If not, there was no telling what the military people might decide to do with the Anomaly.

After a moment's pause, in which Cello's cogitation commenced and stalled, commenced and stalled, certain that she was not mistaken and that Namur was full of shit, but lacking the clarity that would have allowed for plainspoken correction or calling-out, at least not to a degree that would have commanded consensus or even supermajority in the nerve center of the world, Cello merely sighed, sat back in her chair, and withdrew her sidearm.

It didn't seem to bother her that Ogden also produced a sidearm. The guards outside the door were stayed by her upraised palm, which Namur found the most concerning element of the whole scene. It occurred to him that he didn't know who exactly was in charge here. He'd always assumed Ogden was, but he realized this was based on nothing in particular.

Namur found a sharper respect for Lusac when he didn't recoil, didn't so much as a wince, when Cello pointed the black pistol square at his chest.

"I should have put you two in separate rooms. Asked you to state it in your own words, before you had the chance to learn from each other." Her eyes drifted from Lusac's, to Ogden's, to the monitor behind them both, which showed a countdown: 00:04:55:09… 00:04:55:08… 00:04:55:07…. "Please understand and believe when I tell you that, five hours from now, the Anomaly is going to meet humanity for the first time. It will take four hours for transmissions from the meeting site to reach us. Please further understand that if, nine hours from now, I have any sense that a different decision made during this conversation would have improved the outcome, I will take turns perforating you both."

"You will be escorted from the building and court-martialed," Ogden counter-explained.

"I will not," she explained with a tone as smooth as if she had been correcting Ogden's spelling. But, she did return her sidearm to its holster.

Namur could not give anyone else the chance to pick up the thread. "In nine hours, something will emerge from the Anomaly, and we will be united in song." He thumped the table with his wrist and gestured horizontally with an outstretched index finger. "All of us."

He started to stand, but was surprised when Captain Ogden interrupted him. "You are mistaken, Dr. Namur. No more dramatic exits. The Commander is correct. You, and Mr. Lusac here, and all the rest of us, will be waiting here in the Jet Weld building for the next nine hours. Bathrooms are that way, we have cots in the utility room that way, but nobody will be leaving." He rested his eyes on Commander Cello as well. "There will be no more theatrics here. We have orders. Those of you not in the service have contracts. We will all comply with all of the above. Now..."

The meeting changed over into its more administrative phase. Captain Ogden began giving orders and instructions, parsing out the civilians into teams based on areas of expertise, and then directing the military personnel to game out various alternatives.

Dr. Namur and most of the remaining civilians had found space in the rings of consoles around the larger chamber outside of the conference room.

The task of figuring out how to coordinate with the rest of the scientific community, and the wider world, was impossible. Jet Weld was taking in half a terabyte of summary information alone. The chatter and speculation was completely unwieldy from jump. The body was seizing; voltage potentials crackled like fireflies in a damp July dusk. They were cycled through the various floors of the Jet Weld building, hour after pointless hour whiled away on briefings, speculation, synthesis of nonsense into nonsensical syntheses. It felt like the billiard balls the instant after break, chaos in every direction, outcomes knowable, but for Namur and Lusac. They were like water striders over troubled waters, gazing placidly down into the churning foam, gliding on shadows much too big for their little feet.

"What do you think it will be?"

At last, Namur and Lusac had a quiet moment when a sufficient number of bathroom, cigarette, and nap breaks among the scientific and intelligence personnel overlapped by chance, like syncopated harmonies resolving on the same beat. Just enough of a floor was emptied out for them to have what they thought might be a private, or at least a quiet, moment. Lusac's question expressed the only thing that had been on Namur's mind since the end of the first Jet Weld meeting.

Namur finally shrugged, leaning forwards over the railing that separated the peripheral corridor from the central workspace on that floor, his palms curling and relaxing against its cold metal crossbar. "I keep bees up in Blackstone. I might give them lots of different things. Things they might eat, or things that encourage them to reproduce."

"Sometimes people give them smoke." Lusac had lowered his voice, giving Namur the distinct feeling of being huddled in conventicle. "Sometimes people gas them."

"Bees get gassed when they are intrusive, like pests. Otherwise, you like the bees. You need the bees. You want more of them. Fatter bees, busier bees. You know what else you might give them? Nothing, at least not directly. You might plant extra flowers for them, or more hive towers. So that they…." He froze, rooted in place by the ice that suddenly replaced his blood.

"You don't think…"

Just as footsteps indicated the return of some of the workers to their workstations, perhaps the transition from one sleep-scheduled shift to another, Namur broke into a grin, that became a smile, that became bright laughter. He clapped the back of Lusac's shoulder. "Okay. Maybe more than one object. Maybe a *lot* of objects. Fine." His hand lingered on Lusac's shoulder, giving it a gentle squeeze. "Hopefully she won't shoot us both, eh? I don't think she'll mind." He breathed deeply, his face beaming towards the monitor-lit workspace before them. "I don't think anyone will mind one bit."

00:00:00:03 00:00:00:02 00:00:00:01

00:00:00:00 blinked silently on the countdown monitor.

#

The Anomaly received the first deflector. It was a dead-center bull's-eye interception. The deflector was traveling so quickly that the Anomaly was a mere speck of distant light up until right before collision, and then it was almost gone again the instant after, like passing a flickering birthday candle at highway speeds. Had a human observer been onboard, the duration of a blink would have covered the entire stretch of time in which the Anomaly was clearly distinct from the stars in the deep distance.

These fleeting microseconds were plenty for the Anomaly to identify and extract what they wanted.

The Anomaly had full thoughts in those microseconds. It understood the deflector well enough to extract from it their needs in a sequence, and at a speed, that just barely allowed the deflector's internal diagnostics to blare pure panic and critical component 'failure' messages back to the Earth.

The Anomaly found things they wanted, and some things it would teach them to want. The rest it did not need, and would remind them that they did not need those things, either. Almost all of the deflector's momentum was ultimately conserved, the probe buffeted only by the imperceptible breeze of the Anomaly's looking-sense and taking-tools.

Thinking-organ expelled bright waste radiation via capillary effects around the deflector's wire-thin frame, as if caressed by the tiny ripple of air produced by a good-bye wave.

Thinking-organ's messages back and forth with tasting-organ's were nearly instant. Tasting-organ spoke with digestion-extraction, and they were glad.

The Anomaly briefly conversed with thinking-organ and reaction-organ. Processing-organ and analysis-organ joined together to make processor-analyst, and processor-analyst's ensuing efforts were nearly instant.

Its axons conducted thought through uneven neutron electric dipole moments, allowing the charging and relaxation of voltage potentials within the volume of a single neutron; its thoughts were massive, complex, rich, and nearly instant. Wormholes like the Anomaly so small they fit within the volume of individual neutrons conveyed these uneven moments instantly across the whole 'brain.'

Tasting-organ, thinking-organ, and reflection-organ working together means: the body tasted. The body swirled the flavors around its sample-analyzer. Like the flesh of a cherry gnawed from its pit – the flesh being tasted and relished, the pit being unceremoniously discarded – the body allowed the rest of the deflector to continue on its way, less about 12.5% of its mass.

Consumptive-organ had taken the balance through the throat of the Anomaly. Consumptive-organ was grateful to tasting-organ. Tasting-organ was grateful to looking-sense and to the Anomaly. Processor-analyst and reflection-organ briefly conversed, and were glad.

Processor-analyst and reflection-organ glad together means: the body delighted.

Reflection-organ evaluated the overgrown field before it, saw piling wildflowers in the future, smelled the rich emissions of freshly-hewn cultivars, felt the vibrations of the air beneath bizzybee wings fluttering in the distance.

Reflection-organ and processor-analyst delivered the options to thinking-organ personally.

Thinking-organ considered these options over the cavernous span of one full microsecond. Sensing-organ had been listening to the buzzing of the bees for a comparative eternity: weeks, generations spent listening to the bees. Processing-organ and analysis-organ had worked together to generate the range of choices that thinking-organ now considered. Reflection-organ sang to thinking-organ about the bees while thinking-organ thought.

Thinking-organ separated processor-analyst from each other, so it could consult with each of them separately.

#

00:00:16:55 00:00:16:54 00:00:16:53

The four-hour interval between the deflector's interception of the Anomaly, and the near-light-speed return signal was all activity, no action. Jet Weld simmered in a tense silence. At least some of the scientists admitted relief that nothing had happened instantly. Any indication that the Anomaly wasn't subject to the speed of light would have meant that all bets were off – about everything.

Namur had found his way to the highest floor of Jet Weld. He knew they would never have let him outside on the ground floor, but no one seemed to mind him stepping out onto one of the ringed parapets at each corner of the roof level. The building had once been a sprawling manufacturing complex, with OSHA-precise guardrails running around the roof exterior where workers once wove steel into pressure chambers and boilers and other high-end equipment at the cutting edge of a bygone era. Last century's esoteric heavy equipment was mostly gone now.

In about fifteen minutes, Namur expected he would know what materials or equipment Jet Weld and ten thousand strip-gutted manufactories just like it around the world would be revived to produce.

In the distance below, guards marked precise patrol patterns around what had been Jet Weld's parking lot, now a concrete basin walled all around by sandbags and heavy weapons. At every corner of the open roof, anti-aircraft missiles slowly swiveled on their mountings, with drone-searchers panning the sky like tiny searchlights dancing firefly-style against the misty low clouds inaugurating autumn in the distance.

He watched a guard smoke a cigarette. He watched trucks winding precise paths, ferrying the material bases of this-and-that through sandbag channels to feed and oxidize the Jet Weld project. Skin, eyes, proteins, circulation, the body was built, the mind was restive, desperate for something to which to react. The air practically crackled with voltage potentials, as if the ground itself were charged by an impending lightning strike.

00:00:14:05 00:00:14:04 00:00:14:03

Sunrise lumbered up behind dawn's warmth crawling up the face of the mountains. Dew-drinkers came away. Before returning to the elevator, Namur noted the early-riser bees squirming lazily up a copse of peonies growing from the guardrail around the edge of the building.

00:00:12:10 00:00:12:09 00:00:12:08

Captain Ogden orbited the conference room, occasionally stopping to re-inspect the monitor on which the Anomaly and the deflectors were displayed. The second deflector drew ever closer, and would soon be reaching the point at which it would be too late to send it new orders before it reached the Anomaly. They would have only hours to determine what to order it to do – to park by the Anomaly and observe, or to destroy itself and maybe take the Anomaly with it.

"That timer is silly," whined Professor Nelson, who hadn't left the conference room table all night. "There is no guarantee that the Anomaly will have done anything immediately. It might not do anything at all in response to the deflector."

"That would be fine," Petrovic murmured from his perch at the opposite end of the table. "The Anomaly is transparent; we can see the starfield behind it. We'll have imagery from the second deflector at least showing us what happened to the first one. We're taking bets!" He clapped his hands together, gesturing in either direction with his hands at other civilian science personnel. "I say it vanishes. Others think nothing at all will happen to it. Lusac thinks it'll be damaged but intact. How about you, Namur?"

Steepling his fingers, he leaned forwards over the table. "What do you think will happen?"

"Put me down for 'damaged,'" Namur replied with what he hoped was enough nonchalance to come across as guessing.

00:00:10:55 00:00:10:54 00:00:10:53

"The deflector is not the main concern." Commander Cello gave Namur the impression of an octopus relaxing its opsins to drop its camouflage at the moment of attack when she emerged from the dark fabric of her chair. "We have already presumed that the deflector will be lost. Our concern," seeming now to speak royally, though on whose behalf was not exactly clear to Namur, "is what the Anomaly is going to *do*. Not to the deflector, not to the second deflector, but to us."

Professor Nelson had several pieces of paper and a tablet on the table in front of her. By the long and short curves she traced across the paper in pencil, glancing up at the tablet to type in what must have been results to some calculation she was doing. "We will still have more than ninety hours before the second deflector arrives. We do not need to be prognosticating or predicting what will happen or what won't. We will have time for a considered, measured reaction."

"And," Lusac intervened after a glance at Namur, "we must further agree as a ground rule that doing nothing at all may be the proper response. It will all depend on what the Anomaly does."

Captain Ogden walked up the length of the monitor-lined wall of the conference room, swiping his fingers across screen after screen to illuminate them in turn. Each screen displayed a different set of elaborate flowcharts, illustrating proposed responses to different hypothetical next actions of the Anomaly.

"We've gamed out responses to hundreds of different outcomes, from the Anomaly simply vanishing, to discovering that the Anomaly is a strange kind of natural phenomenon, to the arrival of an alien armada. As you can imagine, responses range from doing nothing at all, to launching every missile on Earth straight at the Anomaly," Captain Ogden explained.

00:00:07:24 00:00:07:23 00:00:07:22

"My orders come directly from the Secretary. We will not be giving orders in return – we will be making recommendations only. While this is not being shared with the public, I don't think you will be surprised to learn that there is an unprecedented kind of cooperation taking place among governments right now. The United Nations actually has something to do this week. They are coordinating crisis management on the ground, and preparing to facilitate joint military responses to whatever comes next."

00:00:06:54 00:00:06:53 00:00:06:52

"People are scared. We tried to sit on this, but we knew the word would get out. We cannot hide something like the Anomaly, nor should we have tried. The signal coming back from the deflector is narrow, coded, and direct, but we can't guarantee that only we will hear it. Other governments, other scientists, amateur astronomers working on their own with backyard radio telescopes might be able to see it. Speculation will explode across the internet very quickly. No matter what happens, people will freak out about it, unless we," Ogden looked squarely at Dr. Namur, "know exactly what is happening, and what to tell people. You two," first with a point to Namur, and then to Lusac, "seem awfully giddy about this whole thing. People are already dying. There are suicides. People breaking down, holding vigils, skipping work, taking to bunkers. Not most people, but a few."

00:00:05:44 00:00:05:43 00:00:05:42

"The time for leaving the world in the hands of its most unhinged paranoiac delusions is over." He thumped the table with his free hand, then took his seat. "*Now.*"

Dr. Namur sighed and sat forwards.

00:00:05:30 00:00:05:29 00:00:05:28

Namur realized that there had been a larger voltage potential building and accelerating, piling ionized panic into the adrenal gland of civilization – eight billion adrenal glands aggregated into the shape of a single, larger, much more destructive adrenal gland. The voltage potential would discharge, one way or another. It may discharge down a pathway that engaged the panic-sense, the relaxation-sense, terror or deep quiet breaths.

"The choice is not an even split between investigating the Anomaly, or destroying it. The default position is to destroy it. What I have been told is that, *unless we have a compelling reason to the contrary,* the second asteroid deflector will be ordered to detonate its fusion payload directly inside the Anomaly. That is what we will do if the Anomaly does nothing, because by merely existing, it is already more trouble than it is worth. If that is what you would like us to do, then your current course of action is exactly appropriate," confirming with his eyes that he meant to be speaking directly to Namur and Lusac.

00:00:04:45 00:00:04:44

"More trouble than it is worth!" Namur's suddenly thundering response startled even him. He tried to ignore the hand of Commander Cello, spied from the corner of his eye, reflexively moving towards, but stopping just before, her holster. "Don't let me stop you, Commander. Take out your sidearm, and point it right at me. If I'm wrong about what comes next, pull the trigger."

"I thought we agreed on 'no more theatrics,'" whined Petrovic when Commander Cello actually produced the black pistol from her hip.

"Do not waste the next four minutes." She ignored Petrovic, and did not seem to Namur to seek Ogden's permission or even assess his reaction with her eyes.

"The asteroid deflector will be heavily damaged. Almost certainly disabled, but it won't be destroyed. You will want to interpret this is as a hostile act, an attack on the probe. It is no more an attack on the probe than plucking a peach from a branch is an attack on the tree."

"You think the Anomaly is here to eat us?" came the first reply from a uniform, but Namur ignored it.

"The deflector is going to read as damaged or disabled because entire components will be missing from it. Maybe even the fuselage or its solar panels or some other significant component. Whatever is missing, it will be a single material, like all the steel or all the tungsten or all the lithium. The deflector is already lost. Its telemetry will indicate critical damage to those systems that are removed.

"Shortly after we receive that telemetry, there will be a new and very acute…" he had to restrain himself from saying voltage potential, "panic, you will hear it all around Jet Weld. Because they will detect something emerging from the anomaly. It might be small, it might be large, but it will almost certainly be heading right for us – either for the Earth, or for the second deflector."

00:00:02:10 00:00:02:09 00:00:02:08

"It will not be dangerous. It will be for our benefit."

Namur worked hard to restrain himself from scoffing at Commander Cello's response.

"Are you in league with them?"

Petrovic was not as successful in restraining himself. He repeated the phrase "in league" through laughter, leaning over the table and pressing a closed fist to his face while shaking his head. He didn't even see Commander Cello rotate her body to point the gun at him instead.

"I don't know what, specifically, will come out of the Anomaly. But – and I cannot stress this enough – we will be better off now. All of us. Permanently – forever. Don't you understand? This was already decided four hours ago. The moment the first deflector went through the Anomaly, the stone began rolling and it cannot now be arrested. They sent us the first message. Consuming Otrera was somehow necessary to generate the energy release we detected from the Anomaly. It didn't wait for us to notice it, it announced itself in a way that drew our immediate attention to an unmistakably alien phenomenon. It knew we would see the way it looks at us. The eye of the Anomaly tracks the Earth for that very reason. *It wants us to know that it's there*. No invader would act this way."

Namur hadn't noticed Ogden moving his way around the table until he was close enough to reach over Cello's shoulder and, with a motion somehow swift and fluid but gentle enough to not seem like an attack, pushed her pistol down to the table, its barrel angled towards a corner of the table where nobody sat.

"You will need to convince people outside of this room that we are not looking at invaders here, Dr. Namur." Commander Cello hadn't released the pistol from her grip, even with Captain Ogden's hand on top of hers, nor had she looked away from him. "And if they are not attackers, then what are they?"

00:00:00:08 00:00:00:07 00:00:00:06

Namur searched for the proper term.

00:00:00:05 00:00:00:04 00:00:00:03

"Beekepers."

#

Four hours earlier, processor-analyst had joined with thinking-organ. Thinking-organ considered the options that sensing-organ and processing-organ had generated. Sensing-organ had listened to the whirring of bee wings, and heard many unusual things. Reflection-organ kept the song going while thinking-organ reflected upon the things it heard among the flutter of wings:

Gold, diamonds, chocolate, ichor, platinum, lithium, mom's home!, titanium, nickel, currency, freedom from pain, freedom from want, death, dilithium, freedom from death, return from death, antimony, arsenic, unobtanium, green-leaf volatiles, water, ice, rain, rainfall, gray autumn skies over a light rain on a quiet Saturday morning with nothing urgent to do that day, bronze, brass, mom, tin, red meat, the taste of red meat, the protein of red meat, palladium, calories from all sources, freedom from need, sleep, deep sleep, a quick nap, a quick bite to eat, the smell of her hair, sugar, the smell of his breath, complex hydrocarbons tightly-bound, salt, complex hydrocarbons loosely-bound, the death of my enemies, pewter, the death of my friends, aloe, the death of my love, the death of my parents, the death of my children, antimatter, neodymium, democracy, carbolic acid, children, calcium, iron, love, salvation…

Thinking-organ consulted with analyst-organ.

create category

create category

create category

exclude category: fictional

exclude category: abstraction

exclude category: not amenable to synthesis

Thinking-organ consulted with the storehouse of remembrances.

create category

create category

exclude category: not in inventory

exclude category: can only be retrieved or acquired by exchanges more than three Anomalies away

Thinking-organ pulsed a stream of signals down extensor-organs into the vice-grips and listened for their return calls, like measuring the depth of a deep well by dropping a stone and counting until the thud. Thinking-organ then consulted with processor-organ.

create category

create category

create category

exclude category: every material of any kind that can also be received via exchange with any Anomaly within three Anomalies' travel

exclude category: everything that tasting-organ had tasted on the deflector, including the substances making up the discarded pit

exclude category: every material of any kind which is already abundant in the Anomaly's environment

Thinking-organ consulted with sensing-organ. Together they parsed the buzzing of honeybee wings, and parsed it again, and parsed it again, and parsed it again, until they found patterns, counterpoint, rhythm, isolated the harmony, isolated the soprano within the harmony, isolated the most tender singsong lilt in the harmony, isolated the most thunderous rolling chords in the harmony, filtered out the excluded categories…

…together they wretched at the foul stench of hydrocarbons, the repulsive morning-breath aroma of antimatter...

thinking-organ and sensing-organ shared a joyful laugh.

Finally, thinking-organ chose a reply. One tenth of one second later, thinking-organ commanded relaxation of the proper extensor-organs, which released vice-grips, expelling their return payloads out the opposite way back through the Anomaly.

Together this means: the body opened its palm towards the sky, and cast fresh petals into the wind.

#

The Jet Weld brain was seizing all around Dr. Namur. The sensory-input system was overloaded to the point of collapse. Even Namur hadn't anticipated that the deflector's telemetry, and the response from the Anomaly, would arrive almost on top of each other.

Namur held the seizure analogy, considered it. The firecracker display of data from the outer edge of the solar system surely worked as a form of rapid flashing light. But is Jet Weld epileptic? Its staff of a few hundred had, combined, thousands of years of education between them. It was the densest concentration of Ph.Ds south of Massachusetts at the moment. Even at their most theatrical, the military people had been doing their jobs. Their most gravitational emotions amounted to little more than preparing themselves for the worst.

Perhaps this was not a seizure. This was blinking before bright lights, a momentary recoil eased by a quick blink. The shield between the light source and the optic nerve took the form of Ogden and Cello thundering two simple, alternating commands: "Telemetry! Anomaly! Telemetry! Anomaly!" while pointing here and there, directing individual scientists in ones, twos, and small groups to study the two messages that had come in nearly simultaneously.

One message was the telemetry from the deflector. The second was not a message *per se* – it was the image of some object, smaller than the Anomaly but larger than the deflector, speeding away from the Anomaly.

Namur didn't feel the need to wait for Ogden to assign him somewhere. He found his way to the large bank of computers and monitors on the main floor into which the chattering nervous impromptu telemetry 'team' had been herded. He felt the electricity crackling through the very air around him. When he at last managed to shoulder his way to the largest monitor, he broke into the kind of uproarious laughter that had the same effect of shocking silence into the room that a whistle or a gunshot into the air might have.

CRITICAL COMPONENT FAILURE
THRUSTER TRUSS FAILURE
REACTOR TRUSS FAILURE
PANEL TRUSS FAILURE
FUSELAGE COMPROMISED
YAW CONTROL DISABLED
PITCH CONTROL DISABLED
MAIN BUS COMPROMISED

And, to Namur's relief,

PAYLOAD STABLE
REACTOR STABLE

"Schematics!"

Seniority was no object at Jet Weld, but the perception that Namur had been one of the few on the team who had been allowed into the depths of Jet Weld's nervous system caused attention to fall on his instructions. The sea of shoulders parted around him, technicians fanning out to unoccupied computer stations.

Namur was pleased to see Lusac and Petrovic close at hand, side-by-side by one of the monitors, furiously keying in commands.

"Schematics on your screen now, Dr. Namur." Lusac did not look away from his own monitor, his fingers flying faster than Namur could see. "I know what you're looking for. Calling up the materials list now."

"The materials list?" Petrovic's eyes darted from side to side across a horizontal access with Lusac's face at its center. At last he formed a small smile, as clear a totem as any for the lightbulb that had finally clicked on in his head. "That's why the trusses are reading as failures…"

"They're gone."

Through a chaotic foam of adrenal reflex-reaction faces and noises, Namur and Lusac beamed. Petrovic did not seem to Namur to be capable of forming facial expressions other than frowning, though Namur noted that, at least, Petrovic's frown had become a measure more acute.

Namur thumped his fist and made a triumphant sound when Lusac finished moving the materials list over to his monitor. "Carbon nanofibers. Of course. The asteroid deflectors are modular, same as most other small probes. Different components stitched together on a consistent fuselage plan, similar weights and launch profiles no matter their mission purpose. The layout of an asteroid deflector is basically the same as that of an ice trawler or a tower or a surveyor. The stitches are carbon nanofibers, lightweight but sturdy, multi-purpose…"

"It was going to be that or the steel, right?" Lusac didn't wait for a reply. "I wonder what it's worth to them…"

Namur had one final contribution to make to the hive then. He knew it would be the last ever needed. It would depend utterly upon what the team that had been clustered on the floor beneath his had discovered emerging from the Anomaly.

#

A voltage potential had formed in a new place. It traveled a new path, was charged and released. It passed through the Anomaly and dispersed into our solar system. This excited new voltage potentials in and around the Brookhaven National Laboratory. They clattered and fussed, competing as all neurons do for their share of that scarcest base resource of consciousness: attention.

The mind is a searchlight sweeping this way and that across a roiling black ocean surface, where thoughts and ideas bubble up from deep impenetrable tides of voltage potentials. Each crackle of an ion channel is a bubble rising to its surface. The searchlight falls upon masses or shapes on the surface.

Delegation occurs at all scales. The mind is not a cell or cluster of cells. The mind is the process of the searchlight-sweep and searchlight-fall and ocean-roiling. It is no more an object in the head than digestion is an object in the gut. It cannot be captured in a snapshot, weighed, numbered or measured. It is continuous while attention searches, and stops when the sea is calm.

The searchlight fell upon Namur then. He beheld a monitor. The Namur-searchlight fell briefly upon the thought that life was mostly a sine wave between sleep and monitor-beholding. He preferred to ride the intermediates between the crests and troughs among the bees. He wished he had honey for his coffee.

He did not know exactly what he was looking at on the monitor, but he knew that it was something beautiful. From the Anomaly had emerged a sphere a hair's breadth narrower than the Anomaly itself. Its velocity was incredible along both axes: it approached Mars in a straight line, nearly the speed of light, calculated to intersect Mars's ecliptic so precisely that it would not, per se, land on Mars's surface. Mars would smack right into it as it crossed the plane of the ecliptic.

Already, reflex-organ had purchased enormous gravity for itself. The solar system was littered with asteroid deflectors, all of which had been diverted to intercept the sphere. Fusion payloads were arming, and Mars's pathetic surface defenses, themselves just weaker, immobile versions of the asteroid deflectors, were trained already upon the optimal firing solution to attack the sphere.

Namur was sick to imagine it. Upon Ogden's issuance of the order to ready the species for civilizational reflex-response, Namur had become adrenal. Poor Lusac nearly had to be restrained, for he shared Namur's understanding that to attack the Sphere shared taxonomy with Pontius Pilate, with the teeth in an open palm... Namur felt bees pricking at his wrist. He missed his bees. He longed to see them one more time, and looked forward to being with them forever beginning within hours of his next move.

Dr. Namur understood Captain Ogden. Reflex-response, by its nature, could not be suppressed at the moment of its activation. That pathway existed in a unique position, like mist or steam floating above the roiling ocean, sashaying in the wind without reference to the searchlight, barely reactive to the bubbles beneath. It had to act instantly without attention – but, once noticed, it could be restrained, corrected, reasoned through. That was Namur's last role in this universe now: to contain the outpouring of energy that reflex-response could command.

Only a few hours remained between now and Sphere-arrival. Rapture everlasting, or calamity never before known by any person, would follow Namur's departure from Jet Weld.

Captain Ogden had assembled the de facto project seniors for one final briefing before the commands would be issued that would synchronize a swarm of asteroid interceptors to collide with the Sphere right before Mars's anti-asteroid flak would detonate against its surface.

Namur understood the structure of the Sphere after little more than a glance at the first images to come back from the second deflector. Its surface was smooth as glass, and doubtlessly just as thin. For all he knew, the case material *was* glass. It was the gray cloud inside the Sphere that scared the hell out of reflex-instinct.

The cloud inside the Sphere had the thin, wispy, semi-translucent quality of a gas, but the fine-grain visual imagery had confirmed that it lacked any evidence of Brownian motion. It was like a cloud frozen in time, a painting of a gray autumn sky being dragged through space in a glass sphere. It gave Namur the impression of a snow globe that, once shaken, was somehow frozen perfectly, with its scattering reflective flakes held perfectly still by tiny invisible strings.

"Dr. Namur," began Captain Ogden, his palm already hovering face-down in Commander Cello's direction. "Time is not on our side. The Sphere is traveling almost as fast as our signals do. Only the asteroid deflectors closest to Mars will have time to make the interception. Our command to those deflectors, and to the sixty thousand people who live on Mars, must leave here," he pointed his free hand at a keyboard console on the table, as if the precise point of origin for such a command mattered, "within the hour. Now, this is the situation-"

"You-"

"This is the situation," Ogden thunderously overruled Dr. Namur. "An alien device has destroyed one of our asteroid deflectors. Ignoring the next closest one, it has launched a projectile towards the closest well-settled human planet on an unmistakable intercept course. Barring any reasons to respond the way that anyone who has been shot at would respond, we will shoot back." With that, he settled back in his chair and gestured with that palm now turned upwards. "You, Mr. Lusac, and Mr. Petrovic seem to think that we ought not defend ourselves. If you are wrong, humanity goes from two planets to one at the commencement of its first intergalactic war. Explain why you are so confident that this would be the unmistakably perfect strategic situation for the species."

Namur had had little time to prepare his response, but he saw the hypotheses arranged before him like blueprints. He cleared his throat and rose, moving closer to one of the many monitors running along the back of the conference room. With a gesture across is smooth face, he called up the situation map: a bright circle for each of Earth, Mars, the Sphere, and the Anomaly, with smaller points for the swarming deflectors, and a dotted line connecting the Sphere to Mars.

"Hypothesis: the Anomaly is a weapon; related hypothesis: the Sphere is a weapon and the Anomaly is its delivery system. Aimed not at Earth, whose destruction would represent the doom of the species, but at Mars, who's generations away from self-sufficiency without frequent Terran resupply? Do you shoot back at your enemy by aiming for the head, or by nicking their fingernail?"

"A warning shot," calmly explained Commander Cello. "Show us what they might do to us if they don't detect our surrender in short order."

"An inefficient approach. The Anomaly could have simply opened up over Mars and dropped a million fusion bombs right on its surface. Or they could have sent us a transmission of any kind, something unmistakable. If they are in need of surrendering species, they would not have calmly alerted us to their presence by announcing themselves at the periphery of the solar system, using the most inconsequential object they could find of a size sufficient for us to detect its disappearance. No human habitation within millions of kilometers. Furthermore, to clarify, they did *not* destroy the deflector."

"Ripping its guts out is not a meaningful distinction," continued Commander Cello.

"It is *all* the difference!" Namur drew in one deep breath just fast enough to suppress the next interruption. "Civilization at a certain scale has no need for slaves, or colonies, or protectorates. Whatever arrangement you are picturing that has some political valence to it is utterly anachronistic at the level of interactions between us and alien technologies of unimaginable sophistication. And if the goal is pure annihilation, it is being carried out in a rather foolish manner when the Sphere's trajectory alone indicates an ample capacity for precision with their tools.

"Consider this. The first asteroid deflector was stripped of its carbon nanofibers. What are they? They are a sophisticated industrial product. Quite advanced by our standards, but increasingly ubiquitous. Like steel or concrete, there will always be a need for them. We have had steel for more than three thousand years and we still use it. Not because it is the 'best' material in any sense, but because it is a perfectly adequate solution for lots and lots of problems. Carbon nanofibers are the same way. In three thousand years, we will still be using it *even if better materials are invented later*, because it is relatively easy to make now and it solves lots and lots of problems."

"You're wasting time, Dr. Namur." This time it was Ogden showing impatience. Namur was not pleased to perceive that he was already siding with Commander Cello, and was becoming entrenched by impatience in the reflex-response.

"This is the crux of the matter. The utility of such materials explains why they were removed from the asteroid deflector. It had nothing to do with disabling the probe. It had everything to do with teaching us what the Anomaly is for, and what its designers need – or want – from us."

This caused a murmur of conversation around the table. The assembly was mostly military by this point, leaving Namur with few natural friends in the room. Lusac and Petrovic had already excused themselves from the meeting, pleading the need to continue monitoring the Sphere while the team seniors spoke. In reality, Dr. Namur had them out evangelizing the present mission on his behalf to the other scientific personnel.

"On paper, there is nothing that a vastly more advanced race would need or want from us. They have no need for our spacecraft, clearly. Our best consumer electronics would be of no more value to them than the very best messenger pigeon ever trained would be to a society with portable digital communications technology. And yet," Namur paused to tap some commands on the screen's console, "even societies badly mismatched in terms of technology will always benefit from… trade."

"Please," scoffed Commander Nelson when she saw what came up on Dr. Namur's Screen.

It was a picture of a jar of honey.

"I won't put you through a lecture on Adam Smith," loudly intoned Dr. Namur over the growing vocalizations around him. Voltage potentials…. "Even when one society is vastly more productive or advanced than another, they still benefit most from trade. When the other society invests its resources into making the things that you need anyway, you have resources freed up for other activities. Trade will always be the logical, most beneficial relationship between different societies. A less advanced society might take the roll in trade of supplying the simpler materials, or the less complicated machinery, that the other society needs. It will always be cheaper to buy it than to conquer it, and it will always be more efficient to let someone else do something that you'd otherwise do yourself."

"Alien capitalists," murmured Captain Ogden.

"This is beyond economics. Wealth is a distraction and money is not a meaningful concept here. It is about civilizational efficiency. Aliens that can create wormholes and move them around the galaxy will always have more productive uses for finite labor than primary production. Obliterating another species is not just pointless, it deprives you of a potential source of whatever materials you might need that are at least within the realm of possibility for the other culture. Such exchanges happen all the time. And I'm not talking about exchanges between first-world and third-world nations. We are not a less-developed counterpart to the aliens. We are laggards behind them on a cosmic scale. We are talking about the level of of an evolutionary distance.

"Despite all this, we can be useful trading partners. How can this be?" Dr. Namur tapped the image on his screen. "I keep honeybees at my house in Blackstone. The technology scale between myself and the honeybees is probably roughly equivalent to the difference between us and whoever built the Anomaly. Compared to me, the honeybees have nothing remotely describable as "technology" at all. And yet, I keep them. I feed them and house them, cultivate them like a crop, and in fact I rather enjoy the fruits of their labors."

The din of voices around him began to resemble the pounding of membrane wings against the sky.

"I keep honeybees for honey not because that is the only way to sweeten my tea, but because they honeybees are very good at making tea-sweeter and I can bargain with them on inexpensive terms. They provide the honey because that is what their instinct tells them to do. I provide them with shelter and wildflowers and whatever else a honeybee might need not because I want the bees to like me more, but because it is in my best interest as someone who likes honey."

Dr. Namur ignored sounds from almost all directions when he tapped his monitor over to its next image. He had to raise his voice to continue, realizing that deploying sternness infrequently conferred an artificial air of outsized significance to his words.

"We have already entered into a relationship with these people. I believe that it – the Anomaly, or whoever built it – has communicated with us in the only way it knows how. Think about this civilization, and ours, and all others, as organisms. Those optimally adapted to their environment, those best suited to secure resources for their own consumption, those that form symbiotic relationships instead of predator-prey relationships, those are the ones that will thrive. Such organisms will expand beyond their peers."

Such commotion throughout the nervous system. Namur – a stroke? A seizure? Or the spark of inspiration, the civilizational-neurological result of the lightbulb clicking on?

"This organism communicates with us like this. It likely detected our existence, either through our electromagnetic emissions or otherwise, and sent the Anomaly as a form of invitation. There's no need for more complicated communications; it assumes that any civilization that has achieved a certain level of development will understand what it understands about relationships between organisms. The invitation to trade works the same way that the pistol shrimp and the goby communicate about nearby predators to each other – by instinct, without specific intention, because it is good for them both in a way that enhances both of their survival. Thought and language would be useful, but aren't necessary."

The sound was like a swarm. He felt it rushing past him, the air itself churned into a whirlpool by bodies moving in many directions around him all at once.

"Now, the honeybee produces honey. We have a use for this, even though we have vastly superior technological replacements for sweeteners. We still live with the bees just fine, because honey is always useful. Even at the level of a galactic mega-civilization, basic construction materials like carbon nanofibers will always be useful, *even when superior replacements are available* and *even when they can be manufactured at home*. This way, they get them from us rather than having to do it themselves."

Oh. Petrovic and Lusac had returned. Curious, their faces – ashen.

"Ladies and gentlemen, the Anomaly-builders have received our proposal and accepted it. Whatever is coming to us now, in the form of the Sphere, is their payment."

Namur hadn't even noticed when his monitor had been shut off.

Terramycin Soluble Powder (oxtetracycline), administered thrice daily in dosages of about 200mg, is used to prevent the proliferation of the European and the American foulbroods in beehives. Just two tablespoons, mixed with sugar, can protect a hive for multiple seasons.

Honeybees are known to occasionally mistake Terramycin, and indeed other chemical treatments for beehives, like predators, as if they are tiny insects that have somehow billowed into the hive. Bees will sometimes roll themselves around in the substance and fly away, thinking that they are protecting their hive and their queen by so doing.

Who but the maddest of apiarists would think the honeybee spiteful or evil for doing so? No, the apiarist will simply apply another treatment. Even if the bees prove so vociferous in their rejection of "intruders" like Terramycin that it becomes financially unwieldy to continue treatments, the apiarist has no motive to destroy the hive in some perverse retaliation for natural defensive behavior. No, the apiarist will just leave the hive to its own devices, and hope for the best, should the European or American foulbrood come knocking.

It was only after being returned to Blackstone, again in the black-tinted car, that Namur was told that the decision to destroy the Sphere had been made the moment it was detected. The Jet Weld project served merely to make recommendations, and even if Namur had succeeded in convincing Ogden or, less likely, Cello, that quietly awaiting the arrival of the Sphere would have been the proper course of action, the global military consensus was overwhelming. There was mild surprise that, in the great climactic battle between human and alien, the first single fusion detonation proved more than enough to burst the Sphere, dispersing its contents into a fiery sterilizing sparkler of follow-on fusion detonations. The only weapons on display were those of humanity.

The Anomaly went silent for weeks, undisturbed. It was approached for study, but fusion detonations near or even upon it proved utterly uninteresting to the Anomaly.

With some few further exchanges complete, the body relaxed its vice-grips, and cast further petals into the calm but constant wind.

##

Live By The Side Of The Sea

by

Harold Platte

A Short Story

#

We endured the dying of the Watchlight before Kelvin, finally, decided that he would go to feed it.

Grimly, he began to withdraw himself from the boiler circle. We had taken to sleeping in a circle around the boiler, both for warmth and to have the flicker of its fire to distract us from the Watchlight's own flickering. Kelvin seemed intent on going up to the Watchlight without saying another word. I managed to delay him with a non-verbal croak. We had been sitting around the boiler for so long that my throat was dry from the smoke, and both Kelvin and I each left subtle man-shaped reliefs in the dust on the floor when we rose.

He was stopped with one foot already on the first step up the long, spiral staircase that ascended the body of the lighthouse. One of his palms tightened white around the handrail while the other produced a pack of cigarettes from his pocket. The cigarette cabinet upstairs, on the commissary level that was above the living quarters, kept us well-supplied so I was not surprised to see Kelvin's pack nearly full even though we had not gone upstairs for several days. His lighter, however, had run out, and after flicking it uselessly several times he finally let me light his cigarette for him. Its smoke zigzagged from his trembling fingers.

In morose silence we smoked to the filters. It was only when he was tamping out his cigarette on the long-blackened sole of his shoe that we spoke.

"Still don't think it's a wall." He raised his eyes upwards, apparently indicating the Watchlight, whose dimming light spasmed unevenly across the dull stone interior of the lighthouse. "Just can't take it anymore."

I said nothing. I couldn't even meet his eyes with mine. I understood. The moral arithmetic of it was impenetrable. He was already nearly gone; he'd claimed to have been here the longest among those of us who remained, and he therefore was furthest down the glide-path to decay. I'd seen him tracking the motion of things that weren't there with his eyes, heard him respond to the whispers and groans that he heard far more than the rest of us, all the symptoms we who remained shared but that he now experienced most acutely.

Peter had gone before him, and Peter was nothing but splinters by the end. This roughly established the order of our departure. Length of time in the lighthouse roughly correlated with rate and amount of mental collapse, though Peter's had proven more precipitous, and we all agreed it was because he had gone outside. Nobody held it against him. It was a worthwhile experiment, and we were effusive with our gratitude when he decided to go up to the Watchlight knowing it was his venture outside that had put him there before Kelvin.

Without Kelvin we would be down to five, though we expected replacements to arrive soon enough. Kelvin had claimed that he was tending the wires connecting the dumbwaiter to the fusion reactor when Peter had arrived, and then Elise, then Pablo, then myself, and I witnessed Pavel's arrival. As such, I could at least confirm that Pavel's arrival had been like mine.

The others were unanimous in sternly insisting, perhaps pleading, that I let Pavel – his name not then known to me – sleep as long as possible. It was something of a last kindness, they insisted, and I agreed. The total impossibility of sleep in the first day or two after the first awakening had proven unshakable. Poor Pavel had tried pounding his bald head against the side of the boiler, stooping himself into it again and again like a duck surging its skull into the water for flecks of waterlogged larvae, but this had only produced deep black bruises, and maybe a concussion, but never unconsciousness, no matter how he tried.

And oh, how he tried.

"Anyway," Kelvin continued. And that was it. I returned to the circle of smoke-grayed faces sitting around the boiler and we listened to the dull rhythmic clanging of his footfalls as they died away up each spiraling flight to the commissary, then the living quarters, then the Watchlight level.

Then a silence.

There was a moment in that silence where we all looked around to each other, guilty expressions both for the looking and the facial expressions we wore. Between us all there were two faces only: one which said *maybe this time nothing will happen*, and another which said *please for God's sake let the Watchlight brighten*.

The only sound at the conclusion of his ascent was the slow mechanical grind like the sound of teeth clattering across pavement of the door to the Watchlight opening, and then the softer, almost frictionless glide of the same door back shut. We all held a long inhale, and released it together when light from far overhead cascaded in a great, blazing curtain down the cone of the Lighthouse. Impossibly, cartoonishly, the light expanded down and across the walls scarcely faster than Kelvin would have fallen if he had thrown himself off the railing of the Watchtower level to splatter down here on the concrete floor of the lighthouse instead of feeding it. We had speculated on this, too, without success.

If Kelvin's was anything like Peter's, the Watchlight would blaze bright and healthy for several days before it would, again, begin to flicker and dim. The light offered no comfort otherwise, least of all to Elise, whose face already showed her sullenly mulling over her new place as the senior among us. Now illuminated by the refreshed Watchlight, I could see that a new intensity had replaced the fear I had seen there since I had arrived.

I rested in one of the rusted metal chairs ringing the boiler for some time. Since we were all waiting for somebody else to speak, nobody spoke, and I could only tolerate this for a few minutes before going up to the commissary to start making dinner.

How exactly the commissary worked remained unclear to me. Kelvin and Peter had showed me. Like all the floors it was circular, filling most of the width of the lighthouse with a gap between the edge of the floor and the wall. That clear space between the floor and the wall ran all up and down the interior of the lighthouse, and the unequal size of the gaps between each of the three floors and the wall gave the impression that they had been built at different times, possibly by different builders.

The commissary perimeter was ringed by imitations of appliances but none of them could possibly work. I thought Kelvin and Peter may have already been insane the first time I watched them "prepare dinner." They moved like children, pretending to chop invisible vegetables, adjusting immobile dials on the non-functional appliance-shaped protrusions from the floor of the commissary, pantomiming the preparation of a meal. I laughed out loud when Peter said we could take a break while the food cooked. I remember how startled they both seemed by the sound of my laughter. We did mechanical chores while the food "cooked" before returning to the commissary. Peter pressed the button to send the empty dumbwaiter down to the boiler level, but when we went down there and Peter opened the gate of the dumbwaiter, three plated, fully-cooked hot meals, with water and coffee, were there for us, and I ate in stupefied silence.

Tonight I wanted to prepare something to take our minds off of Kelvin. I couldn't figure out how to tell the commissary that I wanted alcohol. Something brown and cheap that would burn all the way down and make us angry, or make us want to dance, or feel anything other than stupefied defeatism. I worked at it in my mind while preparing the food. While the food cooked I tried pantomiming the unscrewing of a cork, or the preparation of a highball glass with one perfect sphere of ice the way I once enjoyed, or levering the cap of a beer bottle off with the side of the table. I used to open beer bottles with the butt of a lighter, a minor party, but I stuck with the motions that should have looked right.

The food came out exactly as intended, sufficiently rich for enough people that it took the dumbwaiter two trips to bring it all down to us. Plump, pinkish rare steaks, mashed potatoes, and asparagus on their own separate plates, utensils, a couple of packs of cigarettes, all looking and smelling real and rich, except for the disappointing coffee and water.

I made a few, pathetic attempts at conversation but nobody would have it. Pablo ate quickly and retired without a word, depositing his dishes back into the dumbwaiter with a pronounced clatter of frustration, his footsteps up the stairs deliberate with anger. Elise being next in seniority, and Pavel being last, would give them each their own reasons to be drowning in silence. I couldn't even get reactions about Kelvin, or any conversation about the schedule of the mechanical chores.

Partway through my recitation of the order of connections we'd need to stitch over the next few days, something acute and white-hot convulsed through Elise and she surged to her feet.

"What is *wrong* with you?" she roared towards me, and I felt something important in the way that sharp, high-pitched voice echoed up through the interior of the lighthouse slowly, as the light from the Watchlight did.

Since sound travels so much more slowly than light, it was at least two full seconds before the echo of her cry washed down over us like mist falling through fog. Waves propagate more slowly here, I recited internally, though the silence I caused by not responding immediately seemed to make Elise only more agitated.

"We're losing our fucking minds here. Kelvin wanted to leave, too. We have to find a way out. The *real* way out." The way she looked away from me to Pablo and Pavel each in turn suggested a solicitation for consensus. Hearing none, she took a cigarette from the pack she had left resting on the floor by her chair and lit it. Through a cloud that rushed out of her nostrils, she continued. "We still have enough marbles in our heads to do mechanical chores. I'm not going crazy here, and I'm not feeding the Watchtower."

That last part proved striking to me in a way that felt slightly adrenal, the beginnings of panic. Our instructions, such as they were, were unambiguous in this regard:

You must feed the Watchlight with your bodies or the false vacuum will decay and the universe will die.

Kelvin, who must have had a scientific profession before the lighthouse, had tried to explain what this meant.

"False vacuum" was a term of art in a very complicated kind of physics. Its use in our instructions suggested that their author was at least a competent physicist. Together with the incongruous technological sophistication of the lighthouse – which had a fusion generator and a seemingly-magical dispenser of food and cigarettes, separated by a rickety 19th century-looking spiral metal staircase and a water boiler for heat – I suspected that the lighthouse had been constructed by forces of incredible technological achievement who had a childish understanding of humans. While they were for all purposes unknowable, I often thought of them as absent-minded parents.

We also did not know if whatever forces had assembled the lighthouse were the same as whoever had put us there. We never had even a hint of an opportunity to communicate with whomever, or whatever, was responsible for our situation. In this regard the lighthouse was much the same as everywhere else.

My reply felt meek before I even said it, as if it had worn itself out traveling up my throat. "But our instructions say we'll die if we don't."

"We'll die if we *do!*" Elise's reasoning was more emphatic than persuasive. We'd only seen our priors enter the Watchlight room; what happened in there was not known to us. I wondered then if Elise was already starting to crackle apart. To suggest that we let everybody die just to avoid following our instructions struck me as irrational. "Why should we die *now* just to avoid dying *later*?"

I found her question to be distressing. Her tone suggested that she found no sacrifice to be worthwhile, that in principal she should prefer to live as long as possible at the expense of everything else. I was also becoming frustrated that Pablo and Pavel weren't participating. Even quietly acquiescing to the idea of abandoning the Watchlight and our instructions was a betrayal of what I felt to be a compelling moral duty to follow our instructions.

"Because one of us dying now prevents everybody from dying – everybody." I hoped a certain profundity to that answer would buy me the time to begin another cigarette, but Elise continued immediately.

"Bullshit. There is nothing so destructive as what the instructions describe that could be stopped by a lightbulb, even a very big lightbulb-"

Pablo cut her off with an acute grunt when he rose from the circle around the boiler. He started towards the stairs, but stopped by the boiler. He looked at it for a moment, the look of annoyance his face had assumed during the conversation turned to something more serene. None of us said anything when he reached his hand out and pressed his palm flat against the rust-flaked flank of the boiler. There was a hiss of his skin unspooling, the water in his tissues vaporizing and carrying a convection of annihilated flesh into the air. Sharing the stagnant air with cigarette smoke, the lingering flavors of the food, the foulness of human bodies even alive, it filled the lighthouse completely. I imagined that this was what the interior of a long-occupied coffin smelled like.

I squeezed my thumb under the other fingers to suppress a retch, forced to imagine my lungs, like the lighthouse, as polluted chambers now brimming with the fetid fog of Pablo's behavior.

He seemed able to prevent himself from wincing from what must have been intense pain. Nobody moved or spoke until he was finished. When he withdrew his palm from the boiler, little sinewy strings of melted skin briefly connected them together until they separated far enough. With his other hand on the railing he resumed escalating. We at the bottom of the lighthouse watched him go together, eyes following the sound of his footsteps on the cool metal steps as the circled up one flight, then two, then stopped in the living quarters.

Pavel, Elise, and I said nothing for the rest of the evening. We each silently concluded it was best to leave Pablo alone for now so we slept down there without making a sound, except for when Elise briefly went upstairs to "get" some water to clean the charred palm-print from the side of the boiler with her shirt.

#

We awoke to Pablo looking down on us from midway up the stairs. "New arrival. New arrival." I heard him say it several times, each a little louder than the time before it. Without knowing why I pretended not to hear him while Pavel and Elise stirred, keeping my eyes closed and my body curled with my belly facing the boiler. When he reached a "*New arrival*!" pitch I finally sat up.

"When?" Elise was already ahead of us. She had been almost non-verbal when I'd first arrived; her seniority seemed to have awoken, or perhaps reconvened, something inside her, and I wondered if she'd been somebody's boss before coming to the lighthouse.

Pavel and I followed her, but Pablo stopped her at the top of the stairs and pressed his index finger to his lips. "Quietly."

Quietly? "Why?" I whispered hoarsely from behind Pavel. New arrivals were usually so deeply asleep upon arrival that they could only be stirred awake by physically shaking them. Kelvin, Peter, Elise, and Pavel had let me sleep through most of the day.

"It's different," was all Pablo told us. We followed the example of his soft tiptoeing steps back to the second staircase leading up to the living quarters we'd mostly abandoned. The group still used the living quarters when I'd first arrived, but the lowest level with the boiler had proven warmer, and sleeping in proximity to the Watchlight had become increasingly nerve-racking, especially after poor Peter had, in his declining final hours before feeding the Watchlight, suggested that it might be radioactive. None of us believed that it was, but the suspicions Peter planted didn't rely on real evidence for their power over us.

Up we crept, carefully silent. One at a time, as their respective heads rose above the level of the floor, I noticed Elise and Pavel each becoming rigid but not apparently agitated or fearful. They had formed a line a couple of steps below the floor, giving the startling impression that they somehow didn't know how to proceed. When I joined them in the narrow remaining space on that lower step, I understood why, and what I saw made my heart murmur.

The living quarters were six simple beds arranged in a circle around the central spire around which the staircase was wrapped. Four sinks ringed the central spire at equal intervals, though where their water came from or went had proven unknowable. When we still used the residential quarters we hadn't had to assign beds because we simply kept the bed in which we each arose. This system seemed consistent with the lighthouse's instincts, since no new arrivals ever awoke in a claimed bed unless its occupant had gone to feed the Watchlight.

How or when new persons arrived was another mystery to us. Kelvin had claimed that someone who had departed before my arrival had tried to stay up for several days, staring at the one unclaimed bed intently to witness an actual arrival, only to be thwarted when someone had arrived in the span of a single blink.

Our instructions had forbidden us to inquire of new arrivals' former lives. This rule was somewhat self-enforcing, operating more as a mere enunciation of what felt like a natural and sensible taboo, like asking a cellmate what they were in for. I had speculated, of course, building elaborate backstories for these strangers. I might see the roughness of Kelvin's hands, for example, and assume he had been a laborer, or built model ships. Maybe he juggled his pet porcupines.

Upon seeing our newest arrival I turned to look down the row of faces crowding the stair beside me. Something felt vaguely disorderly about the absence of dread I saw there. I felt that a new arrival was supposed to be funereal, a dead-man-walking affair, at best calling for a boring discussion of how to give the new arrival all of the rules. Then the new arrival would have lots of questions we couldn't answer, sometimes panic or anxiety, sometimes a reflexive need to immediately violate the rules. Kelvin had handed down to us a story re-told down through a prior group of a new arrival that had immediately run outside, spent the night there, then returned inside and dashed up to the Watchlight just as quickly as she'd left, and that had been that.

We were already down a couple of spots in the group, and I'd anticipated that this would be the day that they – whoever they were – would start repopulating the unoccupied bed slots today. And they had, though what this new arrival might herald for us proved dizzying even to contemplate.

For there lay, with its tail dangling like the curlicue of an alto clef over the side of the bed, a dozing jet-black cat, its chest visibly and slowly rising and falling with its peaceful deep breaths.

A fog of indecision fell over me. The disconnect between cognitive and executive functions was complete; I couldn't connect any possible action to any possible decision. I therefore felt relieved, fortunate even, when Elise emerged first out of our gathered gaggle. She managed silent footfalls across the metal floor of the living quarters until she was close enough to squat, and then sit, by the side of the bed facing the cat.

The cat recoiled from her, pulled its long paws back against its belly, and rose. It didn't hiss or swipe; it simply turned and bounded off Kelvin's old bed, its paws clacking like little teeth against the metal floor as it explored. We watched it quietly but quickly circle the living quarters floor, stopping only twice: once to give each of mine, Pablo's, and Pavel's stationary feet a quick inspection, and once at the foot of the staircase leading up to the Watchlight.

The cat paused for a moment. Elise, still seated beside the bed, craned her head back to exchange a glance with us, as if trying to gauge what the cat knew or intuited about the Watchlight room. The cat stood and then sat in front of the stairs looking up. It sniffed the air, its erect ears panning side to side across the angle of the staircase. The cat announced its conclusions with a sneeze. It finally toddled back to the bed and mounted it with a silent leap, sniffed Elise's nose, then slumped into an oval and returned immediately to sleep.

We watched in such silence that I had to manually resume breathing when she forwards to stroke the cat's fur. My heart fluttered when the cat stirred, but it only stretched, paws horizontal and spine a closed parenthesis. The cat yawned massively and settled its head back down to sleep. It apparently took the cat a moment to realize something was off, its eyes popping open with a startled incline of its head.

"Ssshh," Elise told it, while slowly raking her fingertips with the grain of the cat's fur across its back. "Ssshh..."

#

While they watched the cat, I watched Elise. Other than the movements of her fingers, she remained completely stationary. She didn't appear even to breathe until the cat, with a deep sigh, nestled its chin against its outstretched front legs and closed its eyes. After several, deep breaths, Elise seemed satisfied that it had returned to sleep. Again with seemingly-practiced silence, she scooted by inches back from the bed before rising and leading us in a slow, silent procession back down to the boiler area.

"This means something," Elise finally whispered, just loudly enough for the rest of us to hear.

"No." Pavel was visibly restless. One of his arched feet bounced one leg, his hands moving up and down his upper thighs through the drab, colorless clothes we all wore. "It doesn't mean anything. None of this does." I noticed Elise glancing upward, apparently concerned that Pavel's steadily rising voice would disturb our new arrival. "Nobody is running this thing, nobody intelligent. It's nothing – nonsense." He gestured with his eyes by crooking his neck one way then the other, vaguely indicating the lighthouse itself. "Our orders were written by madmen or children." He was on his feet now. "They don't know anything. What are we going to do, teach a *cat* the rules? Feed it to the sun, boil it with Kelvin and Peter and whoever else we boiled up for nothing? Teach it how to live and die, how to use a toilet, watch it go insane?"

Elise also rose. I tried to catch Pablo's eyes but he was just staring at the boiler.

Humans can turn invisible. If you've ever been someone who rides the subway, for example, and it's late at night on a Friday, somebody gets on the train at Park Street or Boylston stone drunk and starts making a ruckus, you have a way of tilting your hat down, putting in your headphones (muted so you can retain situational awareness, but it at least looks like you've withdrawn), shrinking into your seat, pulling your backpack up on your knees, taking up less than a whole seat – becoming invisible, uninvolved, like a chameleon, an empty sarcophagus, so that the ruckus would have to manually notice you to see through your invisibility. This was Pablo's look now, and I let him disappear from my visual field for the moment, like letting go of a balloon so it can hide behind the clouds.

I expected Elise to escalate the matter with Pavel, to try to somehow refocus back to her own mad outburst. And yet, "You're right." She spoke it into the uncomfortable silence Pavel had left in his wake, and created a new, tenser silence in which Pavel, Pablo, and Elise seemed all to be plotting.

The situation was spiraling in a way that upset my stomach; somehow, in that moment, I became preoccupied with the question of what would happen if I just vomited all over the floor. Would some system as magical as our food preparation come clean it up?

"This is intolerable," she continued, still using a hissed whisper, as loud as she could make it without overly bothering the cat. "Pavel's right. Whoever put this whole thing together doesn't know what they're doing. They probably don't even know what's happening inside this… place." She had deliberately avoided saying 'lighthouse.'

"So what do we do? Leave?" Pablo had finally joined us, without looking away from the boiler room.

"We're still short. There could be another arrival coming in the other bed any time. We have to figure out if the commissary can make cat food. We don't even know if its a boy or a girl. We don't even know if it can feed the Watchlight!"

My words did not affect the others the way I had hoped. Each of the looks I saw gathered there around the boiler to be different but all equally inscrutable. They weren't paying attention. By how they had lost all regard for the rules, I wondered if they had somehow all gone outside when I wasn't watching.

Elise took a step back from me. The three of them were now a semicircle opposite me. I felt every atom of the distance between us, and the closeness between them. The cat had somehow turned them against not just me, but against the lighthouse, the rules, and the whole world outside. "Wait," nervously raising a hand as if to halt their advance, even though they three were all still, while I stepped backwards towards the staircase. "Just – you can't do this." With both palms outstretched now, I found the lowest stair with the back of my foot and began to ascend.

The moment my foot made contact with the second stair, all four of us winced and gasped with the shock of the light flickering against the walls. The Watchlight was already growing insistent.

“No,” was all Elise could say, first to the others. “No,” she hissed again, to me. “Not yet,” speaking this time to the light on the wall.

I couldn’t stay. They watched me go; I felt their eyes and the direction of their breathing until I reached the living quarters, where lay the cat. Even though I was less capable of quieting my footfalls this time, the cat remained undisturbed. When I sat beside it on its bed it raised its head, made a sound somewhere between a groan and moo in my direction, then lay its head back down. It kept its eyes open, scanning me peacefully, with its paws outstretched so that their tips were nearly right against my upper thigh.

The hushed voices from below that began just seconds after I had taken a seat were animated. I couldn’t make out any words clearly, but I could hear the alternating pitches suggesting that they were interrupting each other, spinning each other up, chattering in agitation. The cat seemed wholly unconcerned, but I nevertheless gave its back several slow strokes with the tips of my fingers. I watched my fingers make subtle streaks in its black fur that closed up quickly. After a moment of this it began to rumble rhythmically, then it listed its side deeper into the bed to show me its belly.

I smoothed my palm back and forth over its belly. The cat purred and stretched, audibly delighted by this. Its fur there was lighter and thinner. The voices downstairs continued with an increasing pitter-patter, timed by the click of consonants and the occasional incline of pitch to cut each other off. Seeing nothing else to do I slowly drew my legs up onto the bed. I was careful not to disturb the cat too much, but even with my body descending across the thin mattress and upsetting the distribution of weight across it, the cat barely looked at me. It suffered my existence in silence, so long as I kept rubbing its belly and stroking its fur.

Noise from below us faded gradually over the next hour or two into part of the ambiance of the lighthouse. They had lost none of whatever energy they had kept for themselves down there, still in alternating argumentative pitches like Gregorian polyphony. Abstracted from content, the sound of three voices in intense discussion was not unpleasant, except to the extent that it may have eventually come to annoy the cat.

The cat and I lay there together, listening to that music and watching the light occasionally flicker against the walls like a campfire over the sound of cicadas. I barely noticed that I briefly dozed off, because my dreams were not sufficiently distinguishable from my surroundings to tell for sure, except that I dreamed that it was dark.

"Is he… *asleep?*" is what woke me up, to the faces of Pablo, Pavel, and Elise all looking down at me from the foot of the bed.

"No," I calmly replied while sitting up.

"Where's the cat?"

I couldn't tell which one of them said it, but it sent a convulsion of adrenaline through me that I hadn't felt in as long as I could remember.

"How did you do it?" Elise's voice was sharp and angular. "How did you fall asleep?"

"I don't know, I was just… patting the cat, and I think I dozed off." They were already speaking over me when I tried to add, "I think I had dreams. One of the doors was open, I think."

Pavel had detached from the other two, peering this way and that around the perimeter of the habitation level to look for the cat. Pablo and Elise seemed determined that I had done something wrong. I wasn't sure when exactly they had concluded that I was evil, or had betrayed them in some way, but the time for disputing that conclusion had passed in my sleep.

"This doesn't make any sense. They sent a cat here to help us sleep?"

"It doesn't make any less sense than the food magic or the light magic or any of the other things that are happening here."

"The instructions don't say anything about a cat. Or humans. It just says 'bodies.' The people who put us here doesn't even know what we are. Whatever comes awake in Kelvin's old bed could be a cockroach or a beehive for all we know."

"It's only been people so far. What did we do differently?"

This last question from Pablo and Elise's frenzied chattering finally gave them pause.

"What did we do differently?" Pablo was tapping his chin now, a crease in his brow suggesting he was trying to assemble the actual details instead of accusing or venting.

"We don't have enough information," Elise said glumly. "Nobody is here more than a week or two at most. We have no institutional knowledge, no way of contrasting our time with prior times. We're always too busy with the, with the-" she flapped one palm beside her head, indicating her own mind and our minds in general, "with the goddamn *racket* of this place." She perked up with an idea. "We need to find something to write with. Some way to pass information onto the next cycles, maybe they can…"

She didn't bother to finish her sentence before separating from us to go downstairs. When I glanced down past Pablo, I could make out her frame standing by one of the "food preparation" areas pretending to write on an imaginary piece of paper. Her shadow flickered briefly with that of the Watchlight.

"Tell me how you slept," Pablo insisted.

"I told you how I slept. It wasn't on purpose, I just-"

He leaned down over me, his knee pressing into the subtle round depression where the cat had slept beside my thigh. "Tell me how you slept! For Christ's sake, I just need an hour!"

"Why are you asking me? I told you. Ask the cat, he seemed good at it."

"'*He*?' How do you know what the cat is? *Tell me what you know!"*

The fact that I knew nothing at all, at least no more than anyone else, did not stop Pablo from closing his fists around my collar and hauling me up to meet him, close enough that his nose nearly touched mine.

Pablo had not been here long enough to have been fizzled out yet, I realized. This was already in him when he arrived.

Taken all in all, I would rather have had more cats than these people.

"Quiet!"

Pavel's voice echoed up from the opposite end of the commissary level where Elise stood. Pablo dropped me, and we both hurried to the edge of the railing to look down at him.

Pavel stood in front of the wide double door that led outside. He was staring into it, with his hand raised up behind us in a gesture that held our noise at bay.

"Be quiet. And come here."

"Did you find the cat?" Elise, sounding oddly hopeful, suggested.

"I… just, come here."

Just as carefully as we had gone up to greet the new arrival, we all quietly descended around Pavel, each becoming very still the moment we heard what Pavel had detected.

It was the unmistakable sound of a cat scratching at the exterior of the door, asking to be let inside.

"What do we-"

"Let it in." There was no hesitation in Elise's voice. She exchanged a look with Pablo and Pavel, then gestured me over to the other side of the door. "Here – stand there, maybe you can catch it when the cat comes inside."

If only I had realized the things that had been growing inside of the people of the Watchlight before I dumbly accepted her instructions. The cat's scratching was rhythmic but forceful, like it was trying to dig its way under the door.

"Ready?" She looked at the other two but not at me, and distinctly waited for both of them to nod back before she opened the door.

By the retreating sound of a croaky yelp the cat made when the door swung open I could tell it had fled, which was my last thought before Pablo and Pavel threw themselves against my back, shoving me out the door.

#

It slammed shut with a terrible noise behind me. I scrambled against it, furiously pounding against it with my fist and calling out to them, desperately. I knew they could hear me; the cat's little paws had been perfectly clear through what felt like heavy wood. I yelled, desperate and pleading. I was never able to muster any anger, only fear, supplication, appeals to decency, and then nothing.

The door had no handle, no crossbars, nothing that I could see that anyone could use to open it from the outside. It was flush against its hinges – there seemed to be no way to pry it open even if I had a crowbar. There was no keyhole or nob. It was weathered and aged, but it looked as if it had been installed backwards, with the doors swinging the wrong direction entirely.

Finally I turned to slump, numb with despair, against the door, and saw for the first time the environment outside of the lighthouse.

A lighthouse is not a searchlight. A lighthouse is meant to indicate the shore, drawing the attention of ships at sea to the position and contours of the shore. It is a warning and an invitation. We had only called it a lighthouse because it felt like one: same general structure, big beaming light at the top, an interior architecture and aesthetic that vaguely conjured New England. Now, outside of the thing and at last distinct from it, I saw that the Watchlight was not like a lighthouse beacon at all. It was a searchlight, focused on some area in the distance lit by a perfect circle of light. Even at its great distance from me I could see that the area it illuminated with its flickering golden glow was scarcely larger than the Watchlight itself, implying that it was an intensely focused beam of light, watching or scanning or highlighting some very specific thing.

As for what was actually within that halo, it appeared no different from the rest of the environment outside the lighthouse.

Black, featureless, utterly black in the shape of an unremarkable landscape having the exact shape of the curvature of the horizon. I couldn't distinguish my hands from the ground, unless I interposed them not between myself and the ground, but between myself and the sky.

The sky contrasted richly with the black earth. It was star-flecked more densely than any night sky I had ever seen. An aurora of green streaked one end of the sky and one of blue streaked the other, like the sky was held up by two great glowing pillars. If there were any clouds they were too thin to conceal the brilliant blizzard of twinkling lights in the distance. The air was so clear and thin that the stars did not twinkle at all, they glowed, and the air had the particular wintertime smell of New England after a snow: wood-burning snow, hints of pine and still water, but if there were trees or snow or anything else on the ground, they were all occulted completely.

I crouched down to touch the ground again. It was smooth as glass and seemed to be the exact temperature of my hand, such that it wasn't obvious that my hand had even reached it unless I applied enough downward pressure to feel my wrist being resisted by it.

And, it was silent. Not silent as in very quiet, but truly devoid of sound. When I was able to calm my breath at last, it was quiet like an anechoic chamber, quiet enough that I am sure I could hear the sound of blood circulating through my occipital vein.

At first I moved in a nervous shuffle, not daring to lift my feet because it would be impossible to detect any obstacle by sight. The movements of my feet were unnatural; it took me several complete shuffled strides to realize that the black environment was nearly frictionless. My movements came to resemble ice skating, except that it lacked the rhythmic sh'rees, sh'rees sound of blades carving a path through freshly-fallen snow.

Having no better ideas, and knowing that my time in the lighthouse had expired, I set off straight in the direction that the Watchlight indicated. I was relieved that after just a few minutes of traveling that the searchlight's radius appeared larger, which I took to verifying by raising my thumb and then both thumbs to measure its apparent width, indicating that it was not so far away that I was at any risk of starving or dropping dead from exhaustion before reaching it.

Nor did insanity take me the way that Peter's time out of doors had led me to believe it would. I had imagined that some outside force had manually destabilized him, and maybe everyone else who went out here, but I imagined that the empty landscape and impossibly ornamented sky could simply seem too strange to comprehend for some people. I found the silence, the perfectly homeostatic temperature, the darkness, and the emptiness of it all to be beautiful, in the way that the desert at night is beautiful only to some.

The light in the distance dimmed and flickered as I expected it to, just as I expected that any moment it would burn back to full strength when Elise, Pablo, and Pavel came to their senses back at the lighthouse. I turned to look back over my shoulder, hoping somehow to indicate an aura of descending orderliness, and I also worried about the cat.

To my stomach-sinking horror, there stood the lighthouse looming over me right over my shoulder. It looked as if I had gotten no more than a few paces away from it after all the time. Back the other direction, the focus of the searchlight remained large. It was as if I had continued approaching the circle of light without ever moving any distance at all from the lighthouse. As an experiment I turned fully around and took one step backwards towards the lighthouse. Over one shoulder, I could see that the lighthouse was a little closer, but the beam of the searchlight was only imperceptibly farther away. It had the appearance of standing right outside of the lighthouse and somehow pulling the halo towards me, as if I were not moving except by rolling a treadmill with my feet, tugging the halo closer without increasing my distance from the lighthouse at all.

This was dizzying to say the least, but I, again, assumed that it was the kind of thing that could drive other people insane, and that I was fortunate to be so level-headed.

I resumed skating towards it. While I did so I occasionally flicked my eyes up from the halo to the sky, trying to contrast their brightness to see if any moonrise or sunrise or other nearer celestial body even existed here. There was no evidence of this. The circle of light in the distance had no powers of glare at all; stars near its perimeter did not dim from my vision in the slightest until they were swallowed up by the beam of light, vanishing instantly without appearing to dim or set or fade in the slightest.

While it was obvious that the light shown against *something,* since it flattened into a circle at some distance without just continuing on forever like a searchlight turned skyward, but like the ground it had no angles or colors or shapes that I could detect at any distance. Part of me worried that it stopped at a wall.

A bigger part of me worried that the light was becoming dimmer and staying black longer, implying that the ones who had stayed behind continued in their failure to feed the Watchlight. The closer I came to the light the angrier I became about what I increasingly felt was a moral failing, a conscious misdeed, a sin against me and possibly something else – deliberate wickedness born not of their fake fears for their own 'lives' (since they had no evidence that entering the Watchlight meant death, nor did they have lives worth preserving anyway), but out of their misplaced, utterly baseless disdain for me personally.

Feed it. You must feed it with your bodies. *You* must feed it with *your* bodies. "Feed it," I finally said out loud, and then again over my shoulder, shouting: "Feed the goddamn Watchlight! Feed it with your goddamn bodies!"

Nothing. Silence, deepened slightly by the uselessness of my anger.

Whatever they were doing there – maybe decaying, somehow dead already; I briefly fantasized that they had found a way to kill each other to force their mutual disobedience – they had deserted and abandoned me, betrayed me, and threw me out into what they at least thought was death in madness. I felt comfortable abandoning them, and that helping me out the door was the only charitable act they had ever taken.

Without them, the universe felt rather cozy. It contained only four objects: there was the lighthouse, which for my purposes was a desolate crypt, and the Watchlight, together with the searchlight by which it illuminated the only conceivable world-line. There was myself. And, somewhere out here in the darkness, there must have been the cat. Its tiny paws would have been silent against the nearly frictionless ground. I couldn't help but imagine it skittering around, unable to get purchase on the world-floor, sliding this way and that.

The cat was nowhere to be seen. Its body being the same color as the ground, I expected to look over and see only the glow of its little eyes in the darkness somewhere. But, the cat did not return to me until I fed the Watchlight.

I passed through the circle of light without realizing it. Nothing stopped the light, it just flattened against the air in a perfectly smooth circle, and I skated through it like passing through a curtain of air. Nothing but blackness, save for two yellow eyes that blinked back at me in the deep distance, lay beyond it.

#

The Watchlight, fully charged, drew in its choice, convulsed fresh life into the waiting beds below, created food, and shone into the deep distance. Kelvin and Peter sat quietly beneath it, unbothered by its brilliant light. The cat paced impatiently back and forth between them, expecting but never receiving the person it had been expecting. That person was gone, fizzled out completely in ways that Kelvin and Peter could never know.

Everyone else was gone, but the Watchlight would replace them. There were no problems at all that Kelvin and Peter could not manage, and it released them back into bed just in time for them and the rest of a full group of six to come awake beneath its thrumming fire.

##

People v. Meriaux

by

Harold Platte

A Short Story

#

People v. Meriaux, 217 Intl. Sup. Ct. 505 (2288)
Excerpted from Farid, *On the Galactic Common Law, vol. 2 – International Law*
Farid, writing for the majority,
Graf, Horance, Brockton, van Mecklen, concurring
Durriffe, concurring in part, dissenting in part (joining in concurrence)
Ruslan, concurring in part, dissenting in part (joining in dissent)
Yan, Chourand dissenting.

PROCEDURAL HISTORY

The Defendant, Raif Meriaux, was convicted at drumhead for the crime of murder. His appeal comes to us through the International Criminal Court, which received the Defendant's extradition and additionally charged him with a litany of violations of the Geneva Conventions. The Defendant, a domiciliary of Luxembourg, faces several further extradition requests from Luxembourg, from each of the nations that funded his expedition, and, allegedly, from the indigenous creatures of 23 Libra(b). These creatures have allegedly communicated their own requests through the vivid hallucinations and nightmares of Meriaux's crew.

The Defendant has not clearly answered whether or not he has received the same requests.

This is a case of first impression on virtually all of its main issues. We granted *certiorari* in order to resolve the many novel legal questions raised throughout this shocking and unsettling appeal.

BACKGROUND

This case, one of first impression for this or any Court, stems from events that have already caused significant political, cultural, and scientific disruptions across the Earth. This Court is conscious of the potentially serious ramifications of its ruling for the future of human space exploration. We will therefore fully restate the factual record before us, which is not materially disputed by any party to this action, including the Defendant, so that our reasoning in this matter may be understood fully in light of the events now being discussed throughout media, academia, churches, and surely every living room on the planet.

In 2285, the *ESA Gay-Lussac* was commissioned by a consortium of philanthropic and scientific non-profits to investigate spectrographic anomalies observed in the ionosphere of 23 Libra(b). 23 Libra(b) is an exoplanet orbiting 23 Libra, approximately 85ly from the Earth. While a lack of accompanying radio signals or other indicators of technological development had made 23 Libra a low-priority candidate for such missions, auditors of data gathered by the Joan Emile Interstellar Observatory became convinced that certain complex energy patterns visible on spectrographic analyses of 23 Libra(b)'s upper atmosphere could be explained by the respiratory processes of then-hypothetical exotic forms of life.

Because this mission was considered to have a low chance of success, and so as to justify its admittedly modest cost, *Gay-Lussac*'s commissioners described it to their funding sources as a standard planetary survey. Information about the 23 Libra(b) spectrographic anomalies was not disclosed to most of the mission's principal investors. As such, the *Gay-Lussac* did not receive, nor did its commissioners solicit, the more extravagant funding allocations that had become typical of other missions specifically launched on missions with a higher probability of encountering extraterrestrial life.

For comparison, the *USS Schumer,* an American-owned vessel which was commissioned to investigate (ultimately-benign) repeating radio-like signals from HD 20781 and deployed less than a month before the *Gay-Lussac,* was equipped with a crew of nearly 80 military officers, a raft of biologists, diplomatic specialists, linguists, communications specialists, and a lawyer with decades of experience in matters of international law. Its multiple redundant Functional Alcubierre Drives ("FADs") ensured that it would be able to travel home for resupply and crew rotations at will. That vessel, which took three years to construct and which currently leases at over €20,000,000 per month (not counting payrolls), was also equipped with a sophisticated long-range sensor array, multiple 720-degree spectrometers, and a two-way ansible communication system permitting communication with Earth nearly in real-time.

By contrast, the *Gay-Lussac* is nearly a century old. It was originally built to move cargo between space elevators on Mars and Earth. Its single FAD was installed specifically for this mission, and was purchased (used) from a decommissioned retrofit of the same class. Its crew of five, inclusive of the captain, were tasked with exploring 23 Libra(b) with hand sensors, a single spectrometer aboard ship, and topographical RADAR. There were no scientific specialists with the crew. Having only a sublight radio transmitter, the *Gay-Lussac* had no chance of communicating with Earth without returning home. The *Gay Lussac* leases for €65,000/month. Its commissioners leased it for two months, and gave its crew strict orders not to return until its mission was one hundred percent complete – so as to save on a refueling charge.

The Defendant is an experienced captain and an accomplished pilot. He had been decorated multiple times throughout his military service to the European Union, and has published several papers on novel suborbital maneuvers in high-energy exoplanetary atmospheres. However, his military career ended ignominiously following a domestic violence charge unrelated to this present action. After this and a number of alcohol-related arrests over the years following, Captain Meriaux found himself taking short-term contracts to make ends meet.

According to the record before us, the Defendant was not briefed on any details of his mission other than his destination and expected travel time before accepting. By all accounts, the Defendant took the Libra 23(b) mission expecting a routine planetary survey of the sort that have sustained him for several years.

The Defendant had been scheduled to spend the first week of the *Gay-Lussac*'s mission studying Libra 23(b) from orbit, followed by five days of planet-side survey. Shortly after arrival, however, the crew came to believe that their topographic RADAR was malfunctioning because of its seemingly impossible outputs. The surface of Libra 23(b) appeared from orbit to be nearly perfectly smooth. Testimony before the ICC describes it as "apparently machined," "featureless," "an ideal shape," etc. (*citations omitted*).

The Defendant and the crew discussed the matter and concluded that abandoning the mission to report what was believed to be a mere malfunction would breach their contract with their commissioners and therefore would forfeit much of their pay. They decided to collect as much information as they could with hand sensors and to explain the matter of the defective topographical scanner upon their return.

The following day, one crew member, Alfonso Lorenz, remained aboard ship to monitor communications and sensors while the others, including the Defendant, all descended to the surface via shuttle. Crewman Lorenz, per the *Gay-Lussac*'s contract, recorded all communications between the crew on the surface below, which were made by radio transmissions between their environmental suits.

The integrity, veracity, and completeness of these recordings has not been contested by any party to this action.

The Defendant and the other three crewmen spent several hours searching for a safe landing zone for their shuttle. Even though the surface of the planet appeared smooth from orbit, unusual weather conditions delayed landing by several hours. Subsequent review of the data the Defendant collected during this initial flyover showed that the complex energy patterns detected from Earth were short, intermittent bursts of extremely dense patches of cloud cover. These clouds were also hot relative to the atmosphere around them, though not electrically-charged. While mostly appearing at random across the planet, these clouds also seemed to form directly beneath Defendant's shuttle anytime an attempt was made to descend within about one kilometer of the surface.

The shuttle's crew ultimately determined that it was safe to pass through these clouds. A spectrographic reading from the *Gay-Lussac* indicated that the clouds were made mostly of water, carbon dioxide, and some more exotic molecules resembling sugar. Even though they were warmer than the surrounding air, the clouds' temperatures did not exceed the boiling point of water and posed no danger to the shuttle. The shuttle's engine exhaust dissipated a cloud formation on their way to the surface.

This Court emphasizes its understanding that the *Gay-Lussac*'s crew lacked both the training and the equipment that would have been necessary to appreciate the significance of this information.

The surface of the planet appeared smooth and featureless from orbit. Records from the shuttle's onboard telemetry systems confirm that the crew made no special or focused investigation of the chemical makeup of the planet's surface, though they did verify that Lirae 23(b)'s atmosphere was breathable and temperate. The crew also took RADAR readings indicating that while the planet appeared visually featureless, it did have subtle topography – shallow valleys and rolling hills whose different altitudes necessitated an active search for a stable landing zone.

It was while the shuttle was making low-altitude flyovers of possible landing spots than Crewman Lorenz remotely activated the audio recording system onboard the shuttle. These vivid and disturbing recordings were made without the knowledge of the Defendant or anyone aboard the shuttle.

Crewman Lorenz had not been specifically ordered to make these recordings. Crew aboard missions of this sort do not normally make such recordings because the data is often redundant with the onboard flight computer and other automatic telemetry, and is generally considered a wasteful use of finite local data storage.

Nevertheless, Crewman Lorenz took this and several other atypical steps to preserve the record in the face of the growing disturbances aboard the shuttle.

The unusual behavior of the three crewmen aboard the shuttle during this low flyover is a subject of considerable debate in the popular and scientific press. By the audio recordings, it appears that significant tensions had arisen aboard the shuttle before Crewman Lorenz decided it was time to begin documenting the crew's interactions. The inclusion of these recordings into the record was not objected to by any party.

Each of the crew agree that Crewman Yolanda Baez was the first to begin exhibiting unusual behavior. While monitoring the sensor console, she reportedly became suddenly and intensely anxious. The other crew later testified that she had become "fidgety." Her testimony before the ICC characterizes her own behavior as "defensive." The Defendant used words like "insubordinate" during his debriefing and in his testimony, stating that Crewman Baez had somehow come to believe that the mission should be aborted immediately for reasons she was unable to clearly articulate. Their disagreement ultimately escalated into a shouting match, and it is around this time that Crewman Lorenz remotely activated the shuttle's onboard audio recordings.

We excerpt Crewman Baez's ICC testimony in relevant part:

Prosecution: Could you please describe this uneasiness that you felt.

Defense counsel: Objection, the prosecution cannot characterize the witness's testimony for her.

The Court: Sustained.

Prosecution: Could you please describe what you felt at this time [immediately prior to the activation of the shuttle's recording devices].

Witness: Many years ago, I was in Armstrong Base [on Luna] with my children when there was a micrometeorite strike near our section. My children were in the next room. The O2 sensor went off. The frenzy to get my children into their little suits… I felt like I was on fire, fire all over my body, and I could only put it out by protecting my children. I don't think I took a breath until their suits were on and double-checked. That was two minutes of white-out terror. That's how I felt in the shuttle at that moment. Desperately afraid... it was an adrenaline overdose.

In turn, each of the onboard crew, other than the Defendant, fell into similar intermittent spells of sudden, acute anxiety and irritability. The audio recordings captured arguments, unnecessary profanity, and sudden inexplicable screams resembling the sounds of night terrors though the crew was awake.

The Defendant does not appear to have been affected by these symptoms. Neither the Defendant's nor the ICC's expert witnesses have been able to explain this.

The Defendant was eventually able to locate a proper landing site without the assistance of the crew, all three of whom had become virtually non-verbal, communicating only with occasional "yelps" and "screams," by the time a landing zone was located.

The testimony of the crew and that of the Defendant begins to diverge at this point. Crewman Baez's version of the story clearly stretches the imagination. She reports that the interface of the shuttle's sensor systems had begun to spell out several dire messages in plain text. Where the

Defendant described the sensor display as showing a normal telemetry readout of the planet's surface, Crewman Baez has testified that her screen displayed the words "DEATH," "LEAVE," "PAIN," "PARENT," and "CHILD," in that sequence and capitalization, over and over again. Crewmen Chell and Gavin, the other two crew aboard the shuttle, cannot verify Crewman Baez's specific testimony, but they corroborate seeing similar messages displayed on their own instrument panels and even in their spacesuit HUDs.

As soon as the shuttle touched down on the surface, sinking almost a meter into the powdery white substance covering Libra 23(b)'s surface, the three crew aboard the shuttle promptly lost what sanity remained. While the audio recordings capture only the sound of their vocalizations, the Defendant has added that their behavior resembled that of children throwing tantrums - rolling around on the floor, banging their fists on computer consoles, and pleading with the captain to abort the mission.

Both the recordings and the testimony of Crewmen Baez, Chell, and Gavin contain unambiguous statements like: "you're killing them!" "We're killing them!"

Chell, Gavin, and Baez each described their respective mental states at the point of the shuttle's contact with the surface as "catatonic" and "blacked out," even though they both stipulate to the authenticity of the audio recordings capturing their horrified screams in perfect detail.

The shuttle's audio recording did not extend to the Defendant's handheld equipment, though it did capture the sound of the Defendant lowering the debarkation ramp and removing a hand scanner from the armory panel. The

Defendant has refused to answer any questions about what he did or experienced in the one hundred eighty-three seconds during which he was outside the shuttle. While he admits that a hand scanner remained behind on Libra 23(b), he objects to characterizations like "left behind," "discarded," or "abandoned," preferring to say that the hand scanner was "taken." The Defendant has not elaborated further. Telemetry and onboard recordings confirm that the Defendant promptly returned to the shuttle and departed for the *Gay-Lussac,* again without the assistance of the crew.

In support of the unusual extradition request we have received from the purported inhabitants of Libra 23(b), the ICC prosecution offered as evidence testimony from the crew as to what occurred next. Some of this evidence is corroborated by onboard recording systems and is not in dispute. Much of it, apart from certain information provided by the computers in the medical bay, is not relevant. What remains, however, includes the words of the Defendant's crew who, in turn, claim to be relaying messages delivered to them telepathically....

[Reporter's note: the Court affirmed the consolidation of these extradition requests into this action, but rejected the extradition requests on separate procedural grounds and found original jurisdiction in the International Criminal Court.]

....By the time the shuttle returned to *Gay-Lussac,* all of the crew seemed to have returned to normal. The Defendant nevertheless ordered Crewman Lorenz to restrain the other three and perform medical exams – at gunpoint. They complied, and Crewman Lorenz was able to confirm that while Crewmen Baez, Chell, and Gavin had returned essentially to their psychological baselines, they retained trace amounts of the exotic sugary molecules that cover the surface of Libra 23(b) in their blood. Alarmingly, he further confirmed that these molecules are sufficiently fine to pass through the blood-brain barrier. But, Crewman Lorenz was also able to confirm both that these molecules were not being exhaled or otherwise exuded by his crew-mates' bodies, nor were they multiplying within them, and so he released their restraints.

At this point, Crewmen Baez, Chell, and Gavin were able to disarm the Defendant, restrain him, and promptly convict him by drumhead trial of the charge of murder. Crewman Lorenz did not participate in this trial. Crewman Lorenz neither assisted in disarming the Defendant, nor attempted to free him before, during, or after the drumhead trial. The other three conducted the drumhead by testifying to each other in support of their conviction of the Defendant, and Crewman Lorenz intervened only to prevent the others from executing their captain by discarding him out the airlock before returning to Earth.

DECISION AND OPINION
Farid, writing for the majority,
Graf, Horance, Brockton, van Mecklen, concurring

The complete record of the trial at drumhead was included in the record now before this Court. The Defendant's captors each testified to each other that the Defendant had murdered the children of Libra 23(b), who, in their early gestational phases, are light enough to float throughout Libra 23(b)'s atmosphere, which in turn caused the sort of anomalies that the *Gay-Lussac* was originally commissioned to investigate. These organisms cover the substantial entirety of the planet's surface, and have evolved to rapidly infiltrate the minds of visitors to their world to warn them against approaching the surface of the planet, for fear of destroying its children, as the *Gay-Lussac*'s shuttle did by dissipating these "clouds" with its engine exhaust.

The troubling implications of the fact that the galaxy is, or has been, so teeming with spacefaring life that Libra 23(b)'s natives have evolved a biological capacity to rapidly identify and infiltrate brain-like structures are not lost on this Court. They are, however, not at issue here.

What is at issue is the central premise of the drumhead trial and the ICC's later conviction of the Defendant: that the Defendant committed murder, either negligently by dissipating clouds over Libra 23(b), or deliberately by landing the shuttlecraft despite the vociferous objections of his crew. The International Criminal Court added several additional charges, including crimes against "humanity." It attempted to quantify the "number" of murders the Defendant allegedly committed through complex mathematical extrapolations from the heat of the shuttle, the size and density of the "clouds," and the apparent density of the surface "dust" covering Libra 23(b) beneath the shuttle's landing struts and disembarkation ramp....

[Reporter's note: the majority rejected the International Criminal Court's further charges on procedural grounds, finding that only the charge at drumhead had been properly received by the ICC Trial Court. The majority further noted that the mathematical calculations used by the ICC Trial Court were speculative at best.]

....The Defendant has further asked this Court to dismiss the charges without resort to the factual record by simply rejecting the validity of conviction by trial at drumhead. We reject this request. While Earth may have been able to largely dispose of maritime criminal law during its industrial phases, the era of FAD travel has fully resurrected maritime law, whose beating heart and soul is the relative alienation of souls at sea from the civility of life on land. We therefore hold that observant application of traditional maritime common law in outer space is legally valid….

[Reporters note: the Court further suggests that such application of maritime law would lead to the dismissal of the Defendant's various civil suits against his crew on theories of assault and battery related to their physical restraint of him. This ultimately came to pass.]

….The Defendant has further asked this Court to reject any use of testimony which alleges to be speech "for," "by," or "on behalf of" the indigenous population of Libra 23(b). They cite to the ancient legal principle that "spectral evidence" – the evidence of dreams, visions, and prophecies – is inadmissible. This Court does *not* hold that spectral evidence is admissible in cases arising from contact with extraterrestrials. This Court *does,* however, hold that testimony does not constitute spectral evidence merely because it is supplied by extraterrestrials. The undisputed record clearly shows that the inhabitants of Libra 23(b) were, in fact, communicating the pleas and warnings of alien life. That such life does not have vocal chords or other tools for the compression and rarefaction of air for the purpose of creating sound is irrelevant. Affecting a witness's brain directly in order to cause hallucinations differs from spectral evidence in the core material respect that it actually happened, and the testimony of all three affected crewmen was consistent across witnesses….

[Reporter's note: the Court went on to confirm that the *reliability* of such testimony remains in the hands of trial courts, and noted that the ICC Trial Court in fact did find such testimony to be reliable.]

What can be known is that three witnesses supplying direct testimony, who were not themselves victims of any crime by the Defendant, nor were they interested parties in the sense of being related to, or otherwise involved with, the putative victim(s) of the Defendant, convicted him of murder. To date, murder has been reserved for humans, with all other forms of the destruction of life described variously as animal abuse or other, lesser crimes. The Defendant has asked us to reject the charge on those grounds.

This Court reiterates that it is conscious of the discussions happening at all levels of government, culture, and society around the eligibility of alien life for inclusion within the moral sphere of human dignity. This Court has been deluged with *amici* on all sides of this question authored by philosophers, theologians, lawyers, scientists, and crackpots. Fortunately, this Court does not need to reach a rule of general applicability in order to satisfy its obligations as to the current case.

In the early days of maritime law, a similar question arose as to whether or not the indigenous peoples of the Americas, or the islands of the Pacific, or other non-European regions were "human." It was variously alleged that such creatures were inferior, subhuman, or even entirely devoid of souls. We now know that the question was entirely misguided, and most of its answers until the modern era were atrociously, in short, ill-considered.

What is clear is that *the inhabitants of Libra 23(b) do not wish to be murdered,* and they communicated that desire as clearly as they were able to the Defendant. It was simply not reasonable for the Defendant to attribute the behavior and pleas of his crew to a sudden, collective madness, or to otherwise treat them as entirely apropos-of-nothing. It is just as obvious that, once the universally-agreed quarantine of Libra 23(b) is lifted and followup missions are sent, they absolutely must be constrained by best efforts *not to murder the indigenous life.*

Had the inhabitants of Libra 23(b) communicated less clearly, or if they had not communicated at all or gone entirely unheard, it is unlikely that the Defendant would now face any charges at any level, from drumhead to this Supreme International Court. But, they did. The Defendant ignored these requests from life that is clearly sufficiently intelligent to plead for its life.

We therefore *affirm* the conviction of the Defendant for murder.

This Court has further been asked, by what purports to be a representative of Libra 23(b) speaking through witness Crewman Baez, to extradite the Defendant back to Libra 23(b) for justice of their own. The testimony of this "witness" as to the Defendant's conduct during his one hundred eighty-three seconds on the surface of Libra 23(b) is included in the record, but we cannot consider this request one way or the other without clarity as to whether or not the "Libran" making this request is a "parent" of any of the "children" killed by the descent of the shuttle, and to what extent this interacts with the reliability of said testimony. We therefore remand the matter to the International Court for the Adjudication of Human Rights to evaluate this testimony as a matter of extradition law....

[*Durriffe,* concurring in part, dissenting in part:

While I enthusiastically join in the majority's conviction of the Defendant for murder, it is ludicrous that my esteemed colleagues would accept the testimony of a Libran as to the murder of a Libran, but would reject it as to whether or not the Librans should be able to punish a murderer for murder. One does not have to be a fanatical xenophile to make the basic inference that, if it is wrong for a human to murder an alien, it is appropriate for an alien to punish a human for murdering an alien. Were I to travel to Japan and murder a Japanese person, I would be guilty of an additional and monstrous moral failure if I were to argue that the Japanese people were unworthy of punishing me for the crime. I therefore dissent from the majority's rejection of the extradition request, while concurring with the conviction.]

[*Ruslan,* concurring in part, dissenting in part:

I concur with the decision not to feed the Defendant, a decorated veteran and a *human being,* to the dust littering the surface of an alien world. This case rests entirely upon the testimony of persons whose brains had been damaged by the inhalation of sugary dust. That such dust is alive at all is an as-yet unresolved question for biologists, yet the majority treats it as already decisively resolved in the affirmative. It is not appropriate for this Court to short-circuit the role of such experts by concluding that not only is such dust alive, but that it is worthy of evaluation from the perspective of hundreds of years of *human* legal tradition.

We know nothing about these "Librans" nor that there truly even are such creatures. Until followup expeditions to the planet are conducted, under controlled and rigorous scientific standards, I think it obvious that all or virtually all of the evidence against the Defendant is spectral evidence at best. I therefore dissent from the conviction, dissent from this effort to backdoor spectral evidence into the common law, concur with the decision not to grant "extradition" to a desolate alien world, dissent from the decision to remand the extradition request to a court of even less scientific competency than this Court, and dissent from the decision to convict.]

[*Yan, Chourand* dissenting:

The majority could not bring itself to identify Captain Raif Meriaux by his capitalized rank. This is their tell: they do not like the Defendant. To them, he is the villain of a science fiction story, rather than the Captain of an insubordinate crew, a veteran and a man who carried out the duties he agreed to perform according the contract he (and his crew) freely accepted.

The majority has forgotten how to overlook the supremely distorting effects of hindsight. Space travel has always been a fraught enterprise. The majority does not have the experience to realize that people do, in fact, sometimes simply lose their minds sometimes in outer space. Space travel is dangerous, long, lonely, and, by and large, it is extremely boring. The creation of a general rule that captains are bound to obey whatever nonsense is emitted by uncool heads among their crew risks permanently arresting humanity's climb up the Kardashev scale by confining us to Earth and cislunar space until the perfectly psychologically stable crew can be manufactured in some future laboratory.

The minority strongly emphasizes that the *outcome* of Captain Raif Meriaux's conduct is not, and has never been, at issue here. The Defendant is not charged with negligent homicide or other, lesser forms of homicide attributable to accident, misadventure, or misconduct. He is charged with murder on the basis of his ignoring the shrieks of less-experienced enlisted crew as if he had run a stoplight and mowed down a gaggle of schoolchildren with his car. There is no evidence in the record that he was ever aware that his crew had been infiltrated by these purported "Librans" until *after* their return to their vessel and subsequent medical examination.

We dissent because we believe that humanity cannot sacrifice its legal or moral principles out of a misguided sense of urgency for amicable relations with whatever beings we encounter among the stars. Functional Alcubierre Drive is a relatively new technology; if alien life is as abundant as has been suggested by the apparent evolutionary history of Libran surface-motes, we will find ourselves reflexively casting ship captains into the clutches of extraterrestrials at the drop of a hat.

Suppose we encounter an alien race which worships oxygen, and regards its conversion into carbon dioxide as a mortal sin. Will we condemn a captain to prison or worse for breathing in the presence of such creatures? The majority suggests that the answer is "maybe," if the underlying testimony is sufficiently spooky. We in the dissent vociferously assert that the answer is "no," not at the expense of human dignity, human legal principles, and human solidarity.

We in the minority stand with and for humanity. The arrogant majority stands for the supremacy of imagined alien law over real terrestrial law. For the future of the species, we therefore, respectfully, must dissent.]

##

www.ingramcontent.com/pod-product-compliance
Lightning Source LLC
Chambersburg PA
CBHW062142160726
48282CB00027B/903
9788197205552